S0-BYV-746

THE KING OF LIMBO

THE KING OF LIMBO

AND OTHER STORIES

ADRIANNE HARUN

SEWANEE WRITERS' SERIES / THE OVERLOOK PRESS

First published in the United States in 2001 by
The Overlook Press, Peter Mayer Publishers, Inc.
Woodstock & New York

WOODSTOCK:
One Overlook Drive
Woodstock, NY 12498
www.overlookpress.com
[for individual orders, bulk and special sales, contact our Woodstock office]

NEW YORK:
141 Wooster Street
New York, NY 10012

The paper used in this book meets the requirements for paper permanence as described in the ANSI Z39.48-1992 standard.

Library of Congress Cataloging-in-Publication Data

Harun, Adrianne.
The king of limbo and other stories / Adrianne Harun
p. cm. — (Sewanee writers' series)
Contents: Lukudi — Accidents — The unseen ear of God—The eight sleeper of Ephesus—Acquiesence—The king of limbo — The highwayman — A closed sea —Heartsick — The fisherman's wife.
1. United States—Social life and customs—20th century—Fiction.
2. Nigerians—United States—Fiction. 3. Students, Foreign—Fiction.
I. Title. II. Series.
PS3608.A788 K56 2001 813'.6—dc21 2001036735

Book design and type formatting by Bernard Schleifer
Printed in the United States of America
ISBN 1-58567-193-2
1 3 5 7 9 8 6 4 2

For Ali, Peter, and Duncan

CONTENTS

ACKNOWLEDGMENTS

SOME OF THE STORIES IN THIS COLLECTION HAVE APPEARED elsewhere in slightly different form: "The Unseen Ear of God" in *Story*; "Heartsick" in *Soundings East*; "Accidents" in *Sonora Review*. "The Eighth Sleeper of Ephesus" won a Nelson Algren award from the *Chicago Tribune* and appeared in that publication. "The Unseen Ear of God" was a first-place winner in *Story's* Short Short competition.

First my heartfelt thanks to Wyatt Prunty, editor of the Sewanee Writers' Series. The MacDowell Colony provided the gift of uninterrupted time. I'm also grateful to the following people for their always insightful efforts in improving these stories: Kevin McIlvoy, Joan Silber, Denise Stallcup, Lois Rosenthal, Robert E. Jones, and, especially, Chris Hale.

Finally I am deeply indebted to Margot Livesey and Andrea Barrett. As teachers, editors, writers, and friends they have no equals.

THE KING OF LIMBO

LUKUDI

NATIFE, PEDALING HARD ON THE BORROWED MOUNTAIN bike, turned onto Old Cross Road and found himself surrounded by a fluttering mass. Wind slid between trunks and branches, coaxing and catching unaware the leaves that leapt from trees like red and gold birds. If he were in charge of the seasons Natife could not have achieved a more admirable effect. It reminded him of the end of summer at home—the burning grasslands, the knobby domes of anthills remaining for memory's sake on the scarred land.

He was resplendent, this tall young man in a silky fuschia tracksuit, a gift from the aunts in Chicago upon his arrival from Nigeria. Fiery autumn light slanted across Natife, flickering on and off as he rode between the thinning trees. Occasionally he passed through a darker grove where, in the shadows between trees, he could hear an amused cackle as the breeze swept leaves up to meet the shimmering air. During those intervals Natife sat upright on the bike, avoiding the underbrush of sound. He gripped the raised handlebars and pedaled determinedly toward Ally.

Already it was the third week of his mission as Ally Reisch's peer counselor, and once again Natife had no idea what he would say to her. It was clear that someone was doing juju on her. Although she was just sixteen Ally Reisch had the pink rheumy eyes and frail blondness of an old woman on her way to bone and ash. What was required was a blood sacrifice. A simple chicken might be enough. If this were a land of tribes, or even of family, someone would do this for Ally. As it was, she had only Natife, assigned by the Chalwright School for extra credit. At least she was no longer terrified by him. The first week she had not said more than a few words, and, failing conversation, they'd eventually drifted to the barn.

In the stable, sweating as she groomed her horse, Ally achieved a rare state of animation. She worked neatly with currycomb and pick, and only then, with her eyes occupied by the task, did she begin to talk to Natife. It was the horse, Denali, who Natife had to thank for Ally's gradual warming. When she was with her horse Ally forgot to be self-conscious, and Natife had perceived shadows slipping down from around her to the plank floor of the barn. Now, after five previous visits, he felt that she held for him a measure of affection. Witness the delicate hug she gave him each time he appeared, a spindly pressure that seemed as unnatural to Natife as the embrace of an insect and yet brought a pale rosy light to the girl's face.

As he neared Old Cross Farm, approaching the cross-road that led out to Moon Lake, Natife came upon two men and a truck almost wholly blocking the narrow lane. One man was tying shut the red truck's rusty tailgate with hard jerking motions. The other was standing by the hood pensively smoking a cigarette as if fulfilling a medicinal rite. Natife had seen any number of such trucks, jacked up and fitted out with enormous tires. He got off his bicycle and started walking around the hunters, noting as he did a dead doe in the truck's bed. Neither of the men seemed to notice Natife. He was almost past when the man at the back dropped the rope he'd been knotting and jerked his head up, sniffing.

"Goddamn!" he shouted. "Goddamn, you stop right there."

Natife readied himself to explain his presence. His back stiffened and an expression of utter neutrality slid like a mask over his normally thoughtful features. After three months in Connecticut he anticipated such encounters. No one expected a black man here in this area of grand estates and considerable lukudi, or *wealthmagic*. At home in the villages people were careful about displaying riches lest they be accused of this black magic and awaken reprisals. But here they were as easy and thoughtless as children piling up a hoard of groundnuts. Estate outdid estate with winding drives and carriage houses, vast groomed lawns and swimming pools, stables, exotic cars, even hot air balloons. It was a veritable themepark of lukudi where a black man seldom held the price of admittance.

The rope-tying hunter wore a red cap with a charging black bull on it and an orange vest that hugged the rounded stomach under his heavy plaid shirt. He barreled past Natife and, reaching the smoker at the front of the truck, snatched the cigarette out of his hand and stamped it into the leaves.

"Just what the hell do you think you're doing?" he yelled. "You're going to kill yourself that way, Pat, and you know it. Is that what you want? Huh? Is that what you want?"

Natife studied the second hunter. He was younger than the first man, maybe late thirties, also red-capped, but the face under the cap was thinner and paler with pinches between the eyebrows. He passed his now empty hand back and forth across his mouth as if to keep himself from crying out.

"You call this a choice, Pat? Dead now or dead later? You're an idiot if you think that—an idiot! Give me your pack. Give it to me, man. And the lighter too. Give me that goddamn lighter that goddamn Denise gave you."

"Ah, come on, Mickey," Pat protested. But the other man thrust his hand out, and Pat dug into the pocket of his quilted orange jacket, pulling out first a crumpled pack of cigarettes and, a moment later, a long silver lighter which he slapped heavily into the other man's hand.

"Half gone!" The older hunter held the pack up toward Natife as if to share his exasperation. "Pat, you're a chump. They tell you at the hospital what will happen, and still you'd do this to your kids."

Pat turned away and leaned down on the truck, his cheek resting on the hood. The other hunter turned to Natife, not seeming surprised to see the boy still beside him, as though he'd summoned Natife to his side for this particular moment.

"Hey, buddy, do me a favor, will you? Take this goddamn thing. Take it and chuck it as far as you can. Or give it to your girl. Just do my brother a favor and get it the hell away from him."

Natife nodded and took the offered lighter. This felt right to him. It had been a long time since he had witnessed brotherhood. The hunter returned to securing the tailgate, and Natife zipped the lighter into the pocket of his candy-colored windbreaker. He gave a prayer of thanks that the man could ask for his aid and, sweeping his long leg over the bike, continued on his way. Minutes later he felt a warm spot pressing against his hip and looked down to see smoke wafting from his pocket. He stopped the bike and reached in for the lighter. As he did so he felt it change shape. Hastily he withdrew his hand. In it came a lump of black coal edged with sparks that disengaged and zinged into the woods. Each time a spark flew, the wind picked up and the brilliant autumn leaves seemed to burst into flame. Natife thought of the hunter, Pat, slumped over the truck, and he moved to throw the coal far away from him. Even as he formed the thought, the coal took on weight and he could not. He set the bike on the edge of the road, then squatted and pondered the flailing coal. A leaf fell on the back of his neck. Between the brushing of another leaf across his cheek and still another on the sleeve of his jacket, the coal transformed again. Natife held the lighter until the silver metal cooled. By then he was thoroughly dazed, and he laid the lighter against his tongue where it burned like a sliver of ice before he returned it respectfully to his pocket.

Ciggy, the horse trainer, was leaning against the outside door of the barn blowing smoke rings when Natife rode up.

"Oh, Christ," Ciggy said when he saw Natife. "It's visiting hour again."

Natife tipped his head in greeting. Sometimes when he passed Ciggy in the darkness of the barn, Ciggy would turn his back or scurry past, his hard hands flapping at his sides, his face averted. Other times the trainer would deliberately stop what he was doing and spout a sentence or two of what seemed an incomprehensible order, followed by an attack of laughter that resembled the cry of a caged animal. "Don't be a fool!" Ciggy had shouted at him once. "They'd take it from you if they could."

Natife paused at the barn door and lifted his bike

over the threshold. The door kept banging shut. Natife struggled to balance the bike with one hand, hold the door open with the other. Ciggy came up close to Natife. His breath made a pattern in the air at the level of Natife's chest. Natife thought for a moment he had come to help.

"What are you getting out of this? They pay you for this? Put something on your scholarship?" Ciggy demanded.

Natife, halfway across the threshold, hesitated to answer, and the door fell back on him again.

Ciggy snorted and watched Natife release his bruised hand from between the door and the bike. "Just keep your hands to yourself," he leered. "This ain't the jungle." He shot the stub of his cigarette into a thin puddle and stalked off, spewing gravel and dust with the tips of his boots.

Natife wondered if maybe Ciggy too was being played with, or perhaps he was a juju man. It was hard to get a fix on him. When Natife tried he saw sullen clouds that obscured the pointed features of the man's face. If Natife could burn those clouds away Ciggy might seem a handsome man—small but well favored by the gods. It was hard to say. The clouds never dissipated but swirled about the little man like dust in a swath of light.

Natife left his bike between the end stall and a wheelbarrow half full of manure and straw and went through the dark barn to the rotted stairs that led to Ally's apartment. The air was thick with fine hairs that tickled his face. Clean-scrubbed leather tack was suspended from nails on the wall like instruments of torture. There were twelve horses in the barn and most of them watched Natife glide between their stalls. One horse kicked at the door of his stall over and over again.

Natife had once seen Ally with her horse in the ring outside. Denali was a monstrous animal upon which Ally barely made a mark. She was wearing a white turtleneck and pale stretchy breeches. Her straw-colored hair was braided into a thin reed down her back. She looked about ten years old. That man, Ciggy, had been there too, holding Ally to the circle with what looked like a long leash, screaming orders that Ally dutifully fulfilled. Even from a distance Natife had seen her heart rising and falling under the thin ribs of her chest. He wondered at the wisdom of leaving her in this place within earshot of that man's demands.

Ally was living in the barn on her father's estate because she had tried to destroy herself with an economy size bottle of aspirin. It was decided by Carena Doyle, the Chalwright therapist, and Burton Reisch, Ally's father, that what Ally needed now was to learn to take responsibility for herself. Burton and his wife, Georgia, had installed Ally in the barn apartment before leaving for London and the theater season. Georgia tried to keep in touch. She sent her stepdaughter packages with cooking utensils and crockery from England as if Ally were a young bride setting up house instead of a wraith of a girl boiling noodles for herself on a two-burner/sink/refrigerator combination in the corner of a stable.

It was Carena Doyle who had come up with Natife. Natife had met with her several times during the summer. The Chalwright School administration assumed that a student as foreign as Natife would find rural Connecticut difficult to understand and that this would lead to instability. They'd had a Polish student once, a brooding sort of girl, who had leapt from the second-floor science room and broken both legs.

At the suggestion of Bernie Kennedy, his faculty advisor, Natife attended several sessions with Carena. He politely watched her move small plastic animals around on her sand tray as she tried to entice him to run his own hands through the sand. This apparently would allow him to "open up" to her and spill his troubles like little shells into the sand. Carena had pink scaly rashes peeling on the knuckles of each hand.

"Allergies," she explained to Natife.

Natife nodded. If she needed help he could supply it. He still found it confusing that no one asked directly for assistance here. Each night before he fell asleep in the dorm Natife could see the pleas of the day, grown cold with abandonment, as they floated among the rooms. What most of them, his fellow students and their pale resident advisor, wanted was to be saved, lifted out of a mire of pain. "I want to go home," he heard and knew immediately that home was not an eighteen-room Colonial in West Hartford. Home, they cried, and Natife squirmed, unable as he lay in the narrow dormitory bed to do more than pray.

On the morning of the third session, Natife appeared with a salve for Carena Doyle, which he gave her, and a dangling charm he hung under the sand table when she went to fetch their coffee. Carena spent that session ignoring Natife. She built a farmyard with a little house for each animal group, and when Natife passed her at lunch the rashes were gone.

Carena ended the sessions and began to think of Nigerians as tender, quiet, easily adaptable people. Natife would have laughed to hear her thoughts. In his family and his village Natife was an anomaly. He was the serious one, as unlike the rollicking rabble of brothers he had left behind as the cool moon was to midday. Nonetheless, it was the image of Natife, sipping his coffee and observing her as she assembled a pigpen in the sand, that came to mind when Carena first heard of the Ally Reisch episode.

In the living room of the barn apartment—oddly shaped like a funnel—Ally and Natife perched knee against knee, squeezed onto the multistriped futon couch in the pinched end of the room. Directly in front of them a cooking show blared on a portable television. The show featured a drunken man who used utensils like the ones Ally stored under her bed. The man made meals that mystified Natife—sauces and creams and layers—in ovens that transformed the food into plastic centerpieces. Natife puzzled briefly about the nature of sustenance. He still longed for the food of his home, spicy crayfish soup with a roll of eba to dip. He wondered if perhaps the daily ingestion of this bodiless food had something to do with the seclusion of spirit in the Americans.

After the cooking show they watched *Guiding Light* and *The Widening Circle* and ate cookies from a bag. Ally picked the chocolate chips out of the cookie in her hand, one by one, then nibbled around it, rotation after rotation until it was gone. Natife approved of her considerate ways though he himself ate half the bag in the time she finished two cookies. The cookies were a great improvement over the Chalwright dining room.

On the screen Roger left Sara Jean for Lana, his ex-wife whom he thought was dead and whom he had never truly stopped loving. Andy tried to take over Manchester Enterprises by deceiving Elyse into signing the deposition that would send Mac, her husband, to jail. The entire Brand clan plotted against Elyse because she held control of Manchester. Natife was startled when Ally said:

"That's ridiculous. California is a community property state. Mac would have half of it in any case."

"You think they are lying then?" Natife asked her.

Ally tugged at her hair, wrapping it around her fingers and pulling, and added the hairs to the little yellowish-white pile she had accumulated on the coffee table. "Not altogether. The hospital seems right.

And the part about the car. But I can't believe the dead wife, can you?"

Her voice was so tentative Natife began to ache. He felt it starting in his chest and hurried to answer her. "It doesn't surprise me," he said. "Some people have memory in their bones and will not die for many lives."

"What do you mean?" Ally said. "Not die for many lives?"

"I mean that some are given many hurdles and must in the end find their right death." He turned to the television to witness Marva Brand peppering Elyse's soup with a poisonous drug.

"Natife," Ally said in a rush, "do you think I could be one of those people? I mean, sometimes I feel like I'm just being pulled around and around the ring with the bit in my mouth, you know. Like, I wonder if I'll ever get out of here or what would happen to me if I did. Like I'm stuck, you know."

Her teeth were picking at her nails. Natife thought that pretty soon she would begin to bite into her arm.

"No," he lied to her. "You are not one of those people."

"Are you sure? How can you tell?"

Usually he and Ally didn't talk so intimately, and this was not the kind of subject Carena would like for him to explore with Ally. He wanted to ask her other questions. "Who," he itched to say, "is after you, girl?" The lighter in his pocket started to hum like a high-pitched electrical wire. Natife hit his nail against it to shut it up.

"Do you hear that?" Ally looked up startled. Natife knew that since she left the hospital her ears would still ring from time to time, always catching her off guard. Sometimes Natife thought he could hear it too, a faint buzz in the air between them.

"It's me," Natife said. He could tell from the wild expression in her eyes how deeply the noise had stung her. For the hundredth time her fragile hold became painfully apparent. She was nothing more than pieces really.

Natife withdrew the lighter from his pocket and hit it lightly again with his nail so that it emitted a soft ping.

Ally looked at it curiously and held out a hand. "Can I see it?" she asked.

What was Natife to do? He watched her as she held the lighter, turning it over again and again with her long white fingers. She read the inscription: "To Patrick, with love, your Denise."

"Oh, this was a gift of love." She sighed. "Where'd you get it?"

"A man gave it to me to throw away. It's dangerous, Ally."

"Life is dangerous," she said quickly and then looked down, embarrassed. "If you don't want it, I mean if you're really going to throw it away, could I have it instead?"

Everything in him resisted. He stared at her. She

was thin as a raking stick, but the lighter had brought a strange heat into her usually dull eyes. He thought: I come to listen but what has she said? What can she say? He had been afraid that when she did speak to him of her feelings it would not be in words but in flashes of light and ice. Who could use such frozen words? Yet for this he had held himself. Like a medicine bowl Natife had been ready to catch whatever Ally would let go, and now the words were forming, ready to spring from Ally's lips in a wild beating cry.

He scrutinized her face. Natife had never seen Ally this way, the eyes, the mouth uplifted, glowing. She was happy, he thought with surprise.

"Take it," he said, realizing that he too felt joy in bringing her a present. He fought off the whispers that gathered in the corners of the room.

On his way out of the barn Natife saw a red glow, the tip of a cigarette, like a firefly in the stall closest to Ally's stairway. He stepped over the threshold and let the big barn door slam behind him before he remembered the bicycle and turned to retrieve it. Even as his hands hovered over the handlebars, an impulse pushed Natife past the bike and on toward the horse stalls. Ciggy was darting up Ally's stairway and didn't glance back to see Natife, standing perfectly still with his hand on Denali.

Other girls knew where to fly when Ciggy swept into the barn, but Ally Reisch would just take it. She'd been fourteen when he first arrived, and she'd stand outside

Denali's stall with her face gone white while Ciggy pressed in on her, demanding precision. The tack she had just hung on the wall was thrown on the ground; a half-full bucket of feed attached to another stall was grabbed and pushed toward her face indignantly as if Ciggy himself were in danger of being shortchanged by the little rich girls. Some of the other girls complained. A few took their horses and boarded them elsewhere. But unlike Ally's other instructors, who'd insisted she work with one horse then another, Ciggy let her ride Denali during every lesson. He showed her how to relax her hands so that she could use the reins to know her horse. "You've got to be loose, baby, so loose you can feel every little change in him." He held her legs tightly so she wouldn't slide back and forth as she posted. "Stay in control," he growled at her. She shook with the alternating commands: "Relax!" "Stay tight!" But she could not walk away: he was giving her a path to Denali.

Sometimes it seemed to Ally that everything had a cost and that she, despite her father's great wealth, was penniless. In the great hall of the stable she wanted to cry out for help. She even thought about turning her back on Denali, walking away for good, but that would be wrenching, beyond what she could bear in this life. Besides, she had nowhere to go. Her debt must of necessity remain undiminished. Ally was all alone and Ciggy knew the exact value of everything that was due him.

Ally moved around the apartment without aim. She couldn't sit still. She couldn't leave. This was her orbit, from the bath to the bedroom to the oddly shaped living room, the kitchen alcove, back to the bath. She was supposed to drive herself to Chalwright three mornings a week but found it harder and harder to go out. Outside, in the car and at school, light slapped at her face, and she felt so exposed her eyes always looked down. She thought with fondness of Natife, how his gentle presence calmed the agitation always vibrating just under her skin. She looked forward to telling him about Denali or to sitting companionably in her living room.

The little room was newly painted yellow. Lemon yellow, custard yellow. In the store on a square of paper it had looked so clean, so new, but on her walls it seemed dingy and tainted. Only one corner of the wall escaped its awful cheerfulness, and Ally came to rest there, half-hidden under the shelves, picking away at the chipped surface. Bits of old paint flicked into her lap as her thumbnail went back and forth. She saw the edge of the hammer above her on the shelf. She had been planning to put up a few pictures after Natife left. She hadn't counted on Ciggy. She reached up for the hammer and hit the wall a few times gently, making a long crack that further shattered the top layer of paint.

The line on the wall opened a memory for Ally, a memory of shelling hard-boiled eggs with her mother as they prepared their spinster dinners on the nights Burton had to rush out of town. Those were the nights when Ally's mother would cry, and they would each eat with their eyes on their plates swallowing half-bites, pretending that the small sobs were coming from somewhere else—like the radio, or a neighbor's dog shut out of a warm lit house. Later, after her mother's accident and after Burton married Georgia, Ally ate dinner with the housekeeper and her husband in front of the television. It was as if she had closed her eyes at nine and opened them at ten, a different girl in a different family, with no memory of how she got there.

Ally cradled the hammerhead. Earlier that afternoon when Ciggy had come into her apartment he had grabbed her by the elbow, reeling her away from the window where she'd gone to wait for Natife's reappearance. She liked to watch him bike down the drive. Ciggy hadn't knocked, never did, and she had barely heard him coming. He had been part of the dust and grime and cobwebs. He had been all over her and she had gone limp and silent.

One day Ally thought she would break in two. She wished she really could become part of Denali. Just disappear into his legs and lustrous brown eyes. She lifted the hammer again. It hit the shelf above her, and the lighter Natife had left fell onto her lap like a star.

Natife came back to Chalwright in a fever, hearing screams. He slammed the bike into its slot and tore up the stairs to his room. His hands ached and he forced himself to write a letter to his father's brother, his second father, a herbalist and doctor, specifying that a goat be killed for Ally. He coated his hands with salve and worked painfully on her fetish. It had come to him that she was the victim of lukudi: the magic that created her father's wealth had come at the expense of others. And one of those others had retaliated by doing juju on Ally. Natife saw the imprint of the little stable man's heels in the dust on Ally's stairs; he heard the wailing in Ciggy's barking laughter. Ally was in desperate need of her own countermagic.

On the way home he had gathered bark and leaves and a shaving from an upraised root. Now he took these and mixed them in his medicine bowl with the nest of hair he had purloined from Ally's apartment and some clippings from Denali's mane. Borrowing a bottle of Gordon's Gin from an upperclassman, he made a libation. He called on first his personal god, then Ally's. He reminded Ally's ancestors of their obligations. He swung and chanted and tried to ignore the rising noise in his room. Breath beat at the back of his lowered neck. He hesitated, then lit a match, and with trembling fingers dropped it into the bowl.

The room hushed. Natife studied the interior of the bowl and sat back on his heels a moment, considering. A question appeared. To go on or let the flame expire? He pictured Ally in her yellow room, cowering and crippled, wasting away beneath swaddled bandages. He added a liquid from a brown bottle along with more gin and chanted again. The light flared. On and on, past the cafeteria's dinner hour, Natife brought in the night for Ally. He saw her grow large and ruddy, saw her stepping high. Ally laughed for him. She ate from his bowl, joyfully, greedily, as if it held a rich and nourishing food. She cleared the fence and disappeared into the night sky, flickering like a star, but it was only when he heard the fire siren, the trucks tearing out toward Old Cross Farm, that Natife caught Ally's cry, caught it as it flew above his head, caught it and held it briefly in his shining bowl. Then he let her fly.

ACCIDENTS

On a Friday afternoon two months after she had fled to Salish Bay, Miranda plowed her car into the porch of a brown gabled house in the uptown district. The house was steep and lonely looking, and when her car hit the concrete foundation the sound reverberated through the still streets like a scream. All through the afternoon she'd been racing ahead, foreseeing every moment of her evening. As she worked her register she imagined herself buying a bottle of cheap Spanish wine. She would sprawl on the sagging couch in her rented house, tumbler in hand, while a television serial beat aimlessly in front of her. She would count the minutes with sips of wine until her eyes could close and she could sink into blankness. Even as she drove down Filmore Street, turning toward Hayes; even as she felt the car erupt with a burst of speed as if overtaken by demons; even as, in the same instant, the brakes failed and the steering loosened; even then the thoughts and images that comprised Miranda had flitted ahead, scouting the territory of the evening and laying the groundwork for her advance. Only when it became apparent that something was very wrong did a summons of sorts go out and all the pieces—the organizing principles of Miranda—return. She found herself clutching the wheel and willing the car toward the house as if magnetized by it.

The impact was tremendous. Miranda felt her skull shift. Her eyes rolled back in her head, the seat belt pulled painfully across her chest, and her right knee knocked against the dashboard. Miranda was no stranger to shock. She knew about disbelief and depression and the beating of one's head against a metal headboard. She sat quietly with her eyes closed, feeling another voiceless scream rise from deep inside, rise and fold outward, a fleeing echo with herself as its source.

Directly above her, to the right of the porch, was a window with the bottom half of a man's astonished face framed between sheer white curtains. Miranda had barely become aware of the man when he disappeared. A second later her car door opened. At first she thought her visitor was a boy, maybe twelve, with a large squarish head. When she finally managed to turn and meet his eyes she saw that he was an old man, in his seventies at least.

"Most people park on the street," he said in a

light, soothing voice. "I can tell you like to do things the hard way."

She could only stare. He began a little game, asking questions. Miranda knew all the answers: her name, the date, even the name of the current president of the United States.

The fire engine came and the first-aid squad. The old man retreated toward the porch as another man took his place, squatting in the open door next to Miranda—a fireman with a clipboard, rubber gloves, and a mask over his nose and mouth.

Six months earlier Miranda's first child, an infant two hours old, had died. The fireman's anxious eyes, visible above his mask, conjured up her boyfriend, Minxter, as he was the afternoon the baby was born, fawning at her bedside, overcome with loving concern. As if Miranda hadn't seen his head turn away from her, from his son, in that telling moment. In the hours before she'd come to the hospital she called everywhere he should have been —his glassblowing studio, the school where he sometimes taught, his friend Eric's apartment. She'd scattered messages like desperate crumbs behind her. Finally she had given up on him and, bent with cramps, taken a nightmare bus ride to the hospital. It was only after she'd been ensconced in a high white bed that seemed to contort with every whim of the nurse that Minxter arrived, bursting into the hospital room clutching a paper bag overstuffed with what he called "our equipment" and wearing a dopey homemade mask that had made her smile at first.

Just as Minxter hadn't approved when she checked out of the hospital early (should she have stayed to make *him* feel better?), the fireman didn't like that Miranda wouldn't go to the hospital now.

"I'm okay," she said unfastening her seat belt.

She half hoped he'd start the old man's game up again: *How many fingers am I holding up? What did you eat for lunch?*

"You'll have to sign a release," he told her.

He had to take off his gloves to peel through the papers on his clipboard for the form, but he put them on again to hand her a pen. Her hand shook as she signed, and her name came out wavy and ragged.

She did not want to leave the car. She cradled the wine in her lap, transfixed by the vision of an old woman hovering above her on the sloping porch, an old woman shuttling her white head up and down as if in agreement. The woman's mouth was open, a tiny purse filled with white teeth. The elderly man who had opened Miranda's car door stood now at the woman's side. His head came just to her shoulder. He smiled almost gleefully. They look as if they won a prize, Miranda thought, and she was drawn with them toward happiness until the pain in her chest and shoulders called her back, and she began gingerly to leave the car.

Slowly, arms shaking, she put the wine on the seat and reached beyond it to yank her handbag off the floor where it had fallen. The fireman helped her put her feet on the ground. Beside her the garden blistered with spring bloom. In the planter, which had landed on the hood of her car, squat red tulips were about to lay open the fringes of their petals. The smiling old man appeared by her side again. He took her hand in both of his, pressed it lightly, and introduced himself.

"The name is Grace, dear, Reiner Grace. And this," he nodded toward the old woman on the porch, "is my wife Laureen."

There was something odd about Laureen's face, Miranda saw now, as if bugs were crawling over it. She felt a twinge. When her mother died of a heart attack, Miranda had found her crumpled on the kitchen floor, dotted with the coffee beans she'd been trying to grind. Miranda never thought to lift her mother to the couch. Instead she sat there on the linoleum beside her, waiting for the ambulance and picking up the coffee beans carefully, one by one. Now, for the first time since her car left the road, with the ambulance lights still spinning and Laureen waiting for her on the porch, Miranda began to panic.

It seemed as if the bushes and signposts were coming to life. The main street downtown where she worked was lined with shops hawking plaster seagulls on driftwood or T-shirts emblazoned with old-fashioned sloops and the legend *Salish Bay*. Even the edge of town was bustling, with its row of taverns overlooking the cannery. But uptown was quiet, mostly residential. Rangy Victorians shared tree-lined blocks with well-kept ramblers and tiny bungalows painted in gay colors. Two corner groceries, a tavern, and a dentist specializing in periodontics discreetly provided the only commerce. From this scene people were materializing—at her elbow, behind the rear fender of her car, just on this side of a tall privet hedge. They gawked and murmured. An obese young man in plaid shorts clicked a camera from the edge of the Graces' lawn. He jogged heavily up to Miranda as Reiner Grace led her toward the porch steps.

"It's for the paper, ma'am," he said. "Can you give me your name, any information?"

"Now, son," Reiner said, "the girl's a bit in shock. Leave her alone. Come back tomorrow, all right?"

Laureen held the front door wide open, and Reiner grasped Miranda again by the arm, leaning a little on her as he tried to help her up the broken concrete steps.

"Just a name then," the reporter called to their backs. "A name can't hurt, can it?"

"Careful," Reiner said. "Easy now." He flattened himself at the threshold to let Miranda go in first, his wife came from behind, and between them Miranda was delivered into the house.

They took her to the left, into the living room. The door shut behind her. She thought she heard a bolt drawn, a latch turned. Miranda was alone with the Graces. Her shoes sank down in the shaggy green carpet. The walls were crowded with framed faces: blond-haired children and sunny young adults caught in careful, smiling poses. Miranda let Laureen put her in a brown vinyl recliner and drape a flowered afghan over her. She started to shiver and she hugged herself tentatively under the afghan. Every movement of her neck shot spasms down her shoulder blades. It felt like wounds reopening. Reiner stood behind her and pushed at the chair's arms until she flew back into a supine position. She resisted the urge to scream and fought against the pain. Laureen brought a glass of ginger ale with ice.

"My mother used to say," Laureen said, "that when you have an accident your spirit flies out of your body and then comes crashing back down into it. The first thing you need to do is get grounded right away. When she had that mishap up at the Belmont— Was it the Belmont, Reiner? Or was it the Chanticleer? You know, Reiner, the old hotel where Gypsy Rose Lee was that one time."

Reiner sat down on the couch and crossed one thin ankle over the other. He looked startled, Miranda thought, and guessed that Laureen didn't often ask his opinion. He closed his eyes as if casting them inward over the past.

"The Markworth, I believe, Laureen," he said.

Laureen leaned toward him, shook her head vigorously, and reached behind him to straighten one of the photographs: a little girl in a fur hat and muff.

"Lord, no, Reiner, they tore that down when we were kids."

She sat on the edge of the sofa peering at

Miranda. Miranda shifted her eyes and found herself staring at a photograph of a young man in an air force uniform.

"Our son Gus," Laureen said. "Reiner took the photograph right after Gus got his wings and before we lost him. Reiner's responsible," she waved a white freckled arm to include all the photographs on the wall, "for all this. Anyway, I do think it was the Belmont. Mother came home and had my brother Hal dig a mud hole in the back yard. She went out and buried her feet in it. Stayed that way for an hour or more till Daddy came home and put her to bed. But she was right as rain in the morning. I don't suppose you'd want Reiner to set you up outside, would you, honey?"

"Your mother—" Reiner began chuckling. "Laureen, your mother—"

"Hush, Reiner," Laureen said. "She hasn't answered. And don't go bringing Mother back into this."

Miranda shook her head, watching the moles dance around on Laureen's face. She was the ugliest woman Miranda had ever seen. Her wide chin jutted out like a shelf below a small pinched mouth. Her nose had the peculiar twist and mold of a foreign vegetable grown unchecked in the garden. It contorted the center of her face, drooping down toward her bow-shaped lips and almost meeting that awesome chin. Laureen's eyes, though, were large and blue, well-shaped and clear—happy eyes that looked amused to find themselves in such remarkable company.

Miranda's hand shook as Laureen leaned closer. The ice in her glass jittered.

"She's cold," Reiner said. "Best thing would be to give this gal something to warm her up and have her lie down awhile."

They wanted her to stay the night, and Miranda, realizing that she had no way home anyway, decided to accept. She doubted she could walk even two blocks. If it was the wrong decision . . . well, hell, it was no news that her judgment often lacked soundness. Over the years there had always been someone—like her Aunt Kay for instance—to point out Miranda's many questionable decisions. After the death of Miranda's mother, Aunt Kay had reluctantly invited the girl to share her garden apartment, but Miranda, with the last tie to home cut, had already been cast adrift.

She set up housekeeping with one poor excuse after another, all sponges, heels, rats. Guys with loud cars and a habit of spitting in the bushes on their way into the house. Miranda felt a dull contentment in these relationships, a sense of rightness. You can't mess up someone who's already screwed up was the way she looked at it. Besides, they left her alone. Not one of them brought her coffee in bed or cobbled together a jewelry box for her the way Denis Minxter had. They blurred her edges and swept her along. All except Minxter. If you were looking for mistakes in Miranda's life, *bingo!*, she thought, you found Minxter. He had overwhelmed her, caught her in a bubble within him. She spoke with his words; his thoughts blew in colored streams through her own. Once he told her she was his whole world. She swore under her breath just thinking of him.

On the coffee table in the Graces' living room sat a huge crystal shaped vaguely like a pointer on a board game.

"Quartz," Laureen said as she stroked a faceted side. "From the caves down in Arkansas. Some people say you should keep a cloth over a crystal this size. They attract aliens apparently. But it's too pretty to cover up. Besides," she added, "Reiner and I always like visitors."

"Not all visitors," Reiner said. "Why, don't you remember—"

Laureen turned toward him again and slightly inclined her head to one side so Miranda couldn't see the expression on her face. Reiner did not continue.

"These are my babies," Laureen said pointing at the photographs. "Have you any children, dear? Is anyone waiting at home for you?"

"She's just a kid herself, Laureen," Reiner said. "Too young for babies."

"I was only eighteen when Cara Louise was born," Laureen said proudly.

Reiner leaned back in his chair. "Yes, well, young people are smarter these days."

"I suppose you think you should have been in New York City or somewhere. On a stage doing those magic tricks instead of here with a wife and a family."

"Well, if you got the babies, you've got to work."

"You're telling me, Reiner Grace."

Babies. The word, the picture, floated around the three souls in the Graces' living room. Miranda felt a heave and a lurch within her. The room shifted from side to side. Reiner and Laureen's voices rose and fell in sharp points. Again Miranda wanted to swear at Minxter.

The baby had come too early. Was it anyone's fault? Minxter said, the doctor said, the nurses said: it's just an accident, just one of those things. The baby had come too early, all in a rush, like a traveler without luggage or money or memory or desire. She had barely made it to the hospital. Even so her labor seemed torturously long, the lights dim in spite of their fluorescent glare. The nurse-midwife came and went, stroking her arm, attaching probes and turning dials, folding linen in around her. Minxter had held her hand and pushed the hair off her face tenderly. He had led her to believe their life together could be flawless, slipping slivers of ice into her mouth, rubbing her shoulders like any loving husband. It was all his fault.

It seemed the world had lost consciousness. The room dimmed with a distant rushing of murmurs, quickened breath, her undeniable groans. As the doctor came in, neat and fresh in his blue-striped shirt, the word came down, and the baby rushed into his makeshift home. They knew right away: one ear half formed, a feeble bleating, no nails or eyelashes, barely even eyelids in fact. Minxter turned away, his face gray, his wild eyes excluding her. His son died less than three hours later. It was all her fault.

That was six months ago. She moved as soon as she could. She fled Minxter's apartment with the newly painted alcove planned for the baby's crib and the glass mobile Minxter had made, revolving like a carousel lost in space. She drove for three hours not thinking, not feeling, just watching the evergreens give way to clear-cuts and back to evergreens again. Once or twice she had been surprised by the brush of Minxter's lips against her own. She'd opened her mouth hungrily before realizing he was gone.

Minxter had followed her as far as Portland. She knew that. She was writing up a sale in the museum store when she saw him through the glass wall gesturing to the security guard, Tony. It would be like him to relate to Tony their whole tear-jerking story. She scrambled out the side door. Next stop Salish Bay.

Miranda managed to tell Reiner and Laureen that she was childless. She didn't cry, but her voice was barely audible. She kept her eyes on the young soldier on the wall. He was freckled and pleasant-looking, and she thought that if he were here, Laureen and Reiner might not seem so strange. Maybe he would hold her hand until she felt strong enough to leave.

Reiner brought her some warm brandy in a coffee cup, and she sat up a bit to take it. As she sipped at the brandy she remembered the wine in her car and wondered if she could get it out before someone towed her car away. She tried to ask Reiner but found she could not speak. Laureen came close to put one surprisingly soft palm on her forehead. Miranda saw the moles on her cheeks twitch. Laureen nodded at Reiner, and together they pulled the blinds and left her to sleep, painfully, in the recliner.

Asleep, Miranda flew gracefully over a great green plain. She drifted over a pristine town of tiled roofs, performing a dizzying spiral around the church steeple that left her weakened and losing altitude. She bumped into the steeple and a piece of slate broke and fell. Below her, white-faced people were gathering, pointing at her, shouting in thin shrieks. A few raised sticks defiantly into the air as if to poke her should she come close. She began to panic and flapped her arms, which made her fall even faster. But then something miraculous occurred. A gust of wind came from behind, and she felt herself buoyed up, back into the non-effort of flying. Minxter appeared beside her, and she smiled at him, holding out her hand. He took it tenderly, and they flew along together past the puddled, angry crowds, over farm fields and lovely blue-green lakes. Minxter flew slightly in front and led her on with encouraging smiles until she looked down and saw only foaming waves beneath her. She lifted her eyes to question him, but he wouldn't look down. He refused to see what lay in store for them. A roaring thundercloud appeared. Miranda let go of his hand to point. Immediately she began to weaken again. This time there was no delay. Minxter was being carried off by the rising wind, carried off in his own patch of blue sky. She called out for him, but her voice made only a small blubbering that dropped unheard into the sea.

Reiner was awkward with the pocket door that separated the living room from the hall. It buckled and banged as he slid it shut behind him. Miranda awoke, not sure for a moment where she was. Her breath was coming in hard gulps, and she concentrated on slowing herself down. Her heart felt painfully large and bruised. Look normal, she told herself. She heard him brush past her and sit on the couch beside her chair. Something touched her hair. She smelled stale cigarette smoke. Her shoes were loosened and removed. Her toes flexed involuntarily.

"You're awake," Reiner whispered.

She opened her eyes.

"Don't let Laureen know."

Together they heard the dishwasher click on and Laureen shuffle down the hall and up the stairs.

"She'd kill me if she knew I woke you up."

"I could use a cigarette," she said. "You haven't got a cigarette, have you?"

"She'll smell it."

"From upstairs?"

"She has a nose like a bull terrier. She can sniff out anything she doesn't agree with."

Miranda caught the merriment in the little man's face, and they both laughed softly. He reached into the piano bench and took out a pack of cigarettes, shook out one for Miranda and one for himself. Wincing, she half rose to take hers from him. They smoked quietly for a minute.

"She hypnotized me, you see."

Miranda stared at him. Her heart began to swell again, pattering against her sore chest.

"To stop smoking. Yes, ma'am, she hypnotized me, but it didn't work, no thanks to her."

He told Miranda how Laureen had sat him down in the recliner and played her tape of rippling streams. She'd turned her ruby engagement ring around on her finger so that, with her palm toward him, the light from the ring shot into his eyes. She moved it toward him and away, rocking his eyes closed, all the while murmuring melodically about numbers and descending passageways. It was like rain drifting into snow, quieter, then still.

"She threw in something about booze too. I like a little bourbon now and then, you see. Laureen thinks it's hurting my health."

"Unethical!" he told Miranda he had wanted to shout when he heard Laureen throw in that suggestion about the drink. But everything in him resisted the sound of his own voice, and so he'd let Laureen go on talking of poison and noxious tastes. That had been more than two weeks ago, and, while they both believed for awhile that the hypnosis had taken, Reiner didn't like the thoughts he'd been having.

"It's not right, this hypnosis, but don't you tell

Laureen I said so. She's still overmad at me about smoking in the first place. I forced myself to start again, though she doesn't know that."

He had started thinking, he told Miranda, that the gap left by being habitless would be filled with something far more sinister to his spirit.

"I know, honey, that smoking and drinking aren't good for you, but I just have this feeling—no, I know it—that there's something much worse in store when you try to make your life fit into all the right boxes."

Reiner blew smoke rings, then shapes. Triangles, diamonds. He blew ghosts of mourning doves. Miranda found herself moving with them, blown between the dusty shafts of summer evening light. Her cigarette burned down. Reiner gently plucked it from between her fingers before he left the room.

When Miranda opened her eyes again, the living room was dark, and the pain in her shoulders rolled and pinched, stabbing the back of her ribs with every breath. She could make out the couch and the upright piano. The photographs weighed the walls down so that they seemed to slope inward toward her.

She found the bathroom behind the kitchen. Her mouth was dry and sour-tasting. She cupped her hand under the faucet and splashed water onto her face. Raising her head she looked into the mirror and remembered the reporter. If he put her photograph in the paper with this address, Denis Minxter would come here. He'd come here and find her asleep in the recliner. She'd open her eyes, and there would be Minxter. Already she felt herself diving back into him, letting him carry her off. Impossible, she knew, impossible.

Minxter once told Miranda that when he was in high school he broke into houses. Although if she repeated that, he'd point out that it wasn't entirely accurate. He didn't *break* into houses; he simply tried doors until one opened. In the Massachusetts town where he grew up, it wasn't uncommon to find an unlocked door and a sleepy Labrador who licked your hand as you groped your way in the dark.

The aim wasn't to steal but simply to spend time in the house without getting caught. No one should know you'd been there. Still, you had to bring something back. Minxter held the record of all his friends. He'd taken a bath and spent half the night on a leather sofa before awakening with the owner's alarm clock and strolling out the back door, carrying only the tags of the winsome Lab.

Minxter said the quiet of a sleeping house was like another dimension, time out of time. Darkness eased every blemish; the houses were always quietly welcoming, like warm caves. In one house he played with puzzles. In another he drank whiskey and perused *Playboy*. In still another he fell in love with a family photograph. "I wanted to be the middle one," he told Miranda, "the boy scout with the sash full of badges."

He had told her, too, about a date he'd had with a girl he liked very much, a volleyball star with well-muscled legs. They'd gotten lucky. A three-story Colonial with a back deck—first try, the sun porch door. The girl had assumed it was Minxter's house. When he said, "Shush, they're all asleep upstairs," she thought he meant his parents.

They made sandwiches and drank Heinekens they found in the refrigerator. On the deck Minxter fiddled with the hot tub until he decided it would take too long to get warm. He kissed the girl and would have done more, but she was not eager to be discovered half-naked by one of his parents. They put their plates in the dishwasher, the bottles in the trash. He was a good son. The girl got something in her eye, and Minxter used an embroidered handkerchief he'd found in a kitchen drawer to wipe the tears from the corner of her eye. He pushed the handkerchief into her pocket. In case she needed it again, he said. It wasn't until they were in the car and heading to the girl's home that Minxter told her it wasn't his house.

"Well, who's was it?" she asked.

"I dunno," he grinned. "Could be anyone's. Could be the chief of police's for all I know."

"We could have been killed," the girl said. "They could have awakened and thought we were burglars and shot us."

"Adds kind of an edge, doesn't it?" Minxter said. He ran his hand up her leg, he said, and she just sat there stunned.

Miranda believed the story. She knew it was true. Just as she knew Minxter would never stop trying doorknobs. Never stop believing in the perfect family, the one she knew didn't—couldn't—exist.

In the Graces' bathroom Miranda fingered a wrapped strawberry-shaped soap in a dish above the sink. I've got to get home, she thought, and wondered what time it was. She stuck the soap in her jeans pocket and decided to find her handbag and somehow make her way to the all-night market where she would call a cab.

When she opened the door of the bathroom she nearly knocked down Laureen waiting for her in the kitchen, ghostlike with her white hair and white dressing gown. Miranda jolted as the bathroom light picked out the deep brown spots wriggling on Laureen's agitated face.

"I heard you get up, honey," Laureen said. "How are you feeling?"

"I think I'd better go home after all," Miranda said. "If I could just call a cab."

"Nonsense," Laureen said taking a step closer. "You can barely stand."

And all of a sudden it was true. Miranda was shaking, one palm against the kitchen wall. She allowed Reiner to lead her up the flight of stairs to a spare bedroom where, moments later, Laureen appeared with a tray. While Miranda ate the vegetable soup and crackers that Laureen delivered, the old woman disappeared into the adjacent bathroom to fill the tub.

"I've made it plenty hot, dear," Laureen said dry-ing her hands on a towel. "You'll need that, I think."

For the second time that evening she pressed her hand to Miranda's forehead before leaving her alone. Miranda waited a moment, then locked the bedroom door. She drank a glass of water and staggered to the bathroom, shedding clothes as she went. Every action took supreme effort, and for a few minutes she wondered if she would be able to pull her T–shirt over her head. Momentarily she wanted to let go, to call out to Laureen. Reiner would come and wait discreetly on the other side of the doorway. He and Laureen would banter back and forth, each of them smiling to themselves. Instead Miranda forced herself to yank at the shirt, gasping as she did.

The strawberry soap fell to the floor when she took off her jeans. She unwrapped it and stepped into the hot bath, easing down gingerly. Her bruised knees stung when the water hit them, and soundlessly she began to cry. She cried and cried. Tears ran down her cheeks and into the water. They filled the air around her with a heady fog distinct from the steam that rose from the bath.

Something in Miranda came unleashed, and she could not stop weeping. She thought of her car and all the places the accident could have happened. She imagined it going wild on the little town ferry, banging into other cars and trouncing truck drivers before flying off the other side and into the bay. She thought of the boulevard beyond the Graces' house and saw her Peugeot careen into the small grocery at the corner.

Children's faces sprung toward her wild with terror. Then she thought of the baby, her baby. His soft cheek against the half-formed ear.

Finally the bath water grew cold, and Miranda maneuvered herself out of the tub. She couldn't sleep. She lay aching in the bed. She couldn't separate the physical pain from her heartsickness and thought to herself, *I can't bear it.* And then, *I sound like a romance heroine—I can't bear it!* What was it she couldn't bear, she wondered, this weight across her shoulders or the emptiness she'd discovered growing larger and more willfully inside her?

The night dashed at Miranda, bringing with it one hurt after another: her neck, her mother's disfigured face, the dark curls on the back of the baby's head that perfectly matched Minxter's as he turned away.

In her fragmented dreams Miranda left the baby on a bus. She fit him into a little boat and went to sun herself, waking to an empty horizon. She put him on the back of her bicycle, rode away, and down he fell, breaking into pieces on a sidewalk scarred with hopscotch lines.

After the last dream her eyes would not close again. Restless, she dressed and, carrying her shoes, unlocked her door. The house was quiet except for a low murmuring that Miranda followed to the room at the end of the hall. She stood in the doorway, in the blue light of the television, and watched Laureen and Reiner. He slept with his head in her lap, again a boy, his feet barely reaching to the end of the couch.

Laureen slept too, her head back, the mouth open and gently snorting. Her arm curled over his shoulder. Miranda could have stood there for hours.

Downstairs in the living room the photographs attracted renegade moonlight spilling through the corners of the closed blinds. Young Gus regarded her with his perpetually cheerful smile. Miranda knocked into the coffee table on her way to pilfer one of Reiner's cigarettes. She glanced down at the wide smooth side of the quartz crystal and just for a moment was sure she saw Minxter reflected there as if he stood ready to catch her should she fall. A new noise, a singular high-pitched whine, whistled through the room. Miranda abandoned the cigarettes and tracked the sound to the front door. Through the glass she saw only the road, washed with moonlight like a gray-blue stream flowing past. On the porch, tilting slightly to one side, she listened. Was it the wind keening through the brambly hedge? The night was still.

Her car was gone—towed away. Without thinking Miranda left the porch and stood in the tracks it had made ripping through the Graces' front yard. Her bare feet sank into the damp spring earth. Suddenly, as if a new sound had come to take its place, the whining ceased. Beneath her feet she felt a slender beat. Miranda forgot her pain and crouched there listening as the nightcalls of insects filtered through the foghorn off Salish Bay. She waited, her hearing newly acute, while the offshore boats answered the foghorn's warning and began to find their way home.

THE UNSEEN EAR OF GOD

TIMMY O'NEILL WAS THE FIRST, BUT THE O'NEILL FAMILY was hardly a peaceful or pleasant one, and the police tsked and put him down for a runaway. John Burton Saks was gone next, along with the family Mercedes (discovered late the following Tuesday by a pair of swamp children who waded through the gasoline shallows to sit in the car's empty leather seats). The police saw no connection in the disappearances; it is doubtful that the possibility crossed a single official mind at that early date. Burton Saks, you see, had a history of trouble brought about by avarice and a boyish sociopathic manner, which might have inspired, so the police thought, visions of revenge. But wouldn't there have been some deeper evidence of foul play than a half-empty package of cigarettes, an expensive foreign brand his family swore he never would have intentionally abandoned?

"Drunk," a detective said, "or worse."

Toby Richler was a different story. Mild, cooperative, a fund-raiser. On a Monday after Little League practice, he sent the others home and went to drop off equipment at the Rec after giving soft-faced Casey Wright a long and private ride home. The call came in at eleven o'clock—no Toby. Scarcely two days later it was Rob Szechwan, the testy hardware man, training for the local 8K run, vanished off the reservoir road.

So who are your suspects? One thinks first of unyielding force. Burly men with guns. Then of unknown habits, commonalities between the missing. Family histories are prized apart and probed. "Could it be terrorists?" the police ask. "Rule nothing out," they tell each other. Mulroon's wife urges him to sleep at the station after hours. He can't bring himself to, but does sheepishly initiate a carpool—at first just for men who leave work when it's dark. Then, when the guy at the gym is carried off in broad daylight with no witnesses, the van starts operating full time. The side effects of men grouping are amazing. The streets of town resound with a pure and willing emptiness. Women and children, after a period of shying away, reclaim them. Before long it is not uncommon to see a lone child, say a ten-year-old girl, sprawled on the grass of the courthouse lawn, watching the stars with a calm radiance that must be rapture.

Jenny O'Neill, for the first time in her life, is tasting peace. Sure, she misses her dad. The dad who twirled her in a swooping arc out over the Rec pool, the dad who called her Tootsle, and whose hand upon her head made her warm with pleasure. But let's be honest. Jenny, young though she is, has been missing that dad for years. In contrast she is celebrating the blessed removal of that other man who, tired of the scramble of work and his ever-needy family, screamed at her mother and her and even especially her tiny brother, Jamie of the Frequent Earache. The man who broke her mother's favorite plate and yelled at Jenny for crying, so that he had to twist her arm and shake her until she'd lost her breath and fainted. The freedom that has come with her father's absence is excruciatingly delightful. "Go play, Jenny," her mother tells her with a smile. "It's all right." Her mother herself has lost years. She dresses in light tanks and shorts and takes long runs in the blue-washed moonlight.

On a hillside to the north of town, an ancient convent carries on its daily routines as if time does not exist. Season follows season in a predictable march for which the sisters, if they consider the flush of time at all, feel a satisfied gratitude. Inside the crumbling, mice-ridden walls, floors are shined, linen is bleached, and prayers are said in response to the bundle of pleas that arrive daily in the mail, folded around checks. A contingent of nuns sorts the letters and replies to them in short typewritten notes: *Our prayers are with your Thomas and his new wife during this difficult time. We include your dear aunt, Germaine, in our prayers. May*

God hear our prayers for her speedy recovery. These particular nuns, it is felt, hold a special position, raised on their toes and pressed against the unseen ear of God. Nonetheless, the honor of their proximity to Him has done little to swell their ranks. The last novices arrived some twenty years ago during a heat wave that was still blamed for the tragedy.

A young sister, Babiana, who'd toyed with both the Carmelites and the Little Sisters of the Poor before committing to this contemplative order, was out wandering in the evening, searching for a bit of a breeze. The avenue in those days was well maintained, the grottos unchipped and filled with flowers. But Babiana chose a trail between tall grasses, under the green lace of budding ash trees. It was her spot, a private getaway where her thoughts seemed to rush and bubble with the winter-released stream. The man who'd met her at the shore was from the town. A hard worker, you could guess, pushed to the brink, gone weak in the head from the oppressive heat. He came out from behind the bushes with a harsh noise that made her spring from her seat on the rock. She promised him anything, even salvation, if he would let her be. But he could not, and later, much later, after a long twilight-to-dawn search, they found her weighted to the bosom of the river, a victim of her own hand. Poor crazy nun.

There are rumors around the mill, the station, the café, that a militant band of feminists is responsible. Even the Sisters are suspect. Yet in the café the waitresses pooh-pooh the men's farfetched conjectures. Big Janice Krause, who works the morning counter shift, slops coffee into stained white mugs and makes disparaging remarks about the speakers' masculinity. Remarks that are taken up by the other waitresses and even the far corner table of courthouse secretaries. Remarks that hit home. For all the bravado, impotence is going around. More than once the water source of town is mentioned, and testing is promised as soon as enough men are willing to make the trip out to the lonely reservoir. At a town meeting even those men who have in the past voiced the smallest of grievances find themselves reluctant to speak. Wives pat down startled hands, stroke hairy forearms rigid with tension. Finally, Mrs. Luke Weber, the mayor's wife, directs the group's attention to the back of the room where refreshments are laid out and several council members are already standing, cups grown cold in their hands, expressions of anxiety molded around their cookie-filled cheeks.

And who *is* responsible? All the criminal texts and television murder mysteries would lead one to ask what is sometimes termed "The Question of the Will." To whose great gain have come quiet nights and still woods where even a fragile leaf of a girl can linger unmolested? Jenny learns her prayers at Sunday School from that little wren, Marta Richler, wife of the missing Little League coach. "Please, God," she prays dutifully, "let them be found safe and unharmed." Then she adds a prayer all of her own making, a prayer that is repeated silently in almost every household in the town.

THE EIGHTH SLEEPER OF EPHESUS

At the moment the apple, lobbed on a dare, began its trajectory toward one of the upstairs windows of his house, Frank Cocokowski was dreaming he was wedged across the bottom of a deep well. Half awake, the way he sometimes was in his dreams, Frank was pissed off. He had spent hours trying to fall asleep, baiting himself with milk and the drone of the television, only to be trapped in this dark corner of a dream.

Had he fallen or had someone brought him to this hard nest? His leg *was* bent unnaturally to one side and his palms, held upward as if in supplication, were stinging, but despite the great distance between himself and the rest of the world, he wasn't utterly in the dark. Far above him the palest of blue skies winked like a distant sea. A circle of light bounced momentarily across his pajama legs, then disappeared. A moment later an enormous disk of coppery gold whacked Frank directly in the center of his chest. Even in his dream he heard his body—the real one—expel a windy, surprised grunt.

"Bingo!" his dead wife Sheila called out. "Gotcha!"

Don't shout in my ear! Frank tried to shout back. He was too tired to form the words and garbled something that sounded like *don shue.* Besides, he was overcome by the task of removing himself from under the fallen object, which turned out to be nothing more than a bright penny of astonishingly normal size. Sheila's giddy laugh rang against the stone walls and woke Frank just as a wave of cold air entered his bedroom.

The apple landed in his son Kevin's old bedroom and, although dusted with glass, was remarkably unscathed: a lustrous, seemingly perfect, fairy-tale apple stuck to the wool carpet. The center of Kevin's room sparkled with tiny bits of glass. As he peered tentatively from the lit hallway, Frank had the strange sensation that something was alive in there. Ludicrous, he knew. All of Kevin's pets—the turtles, gerbils, and lizards—were gone, as of course was Kevin.

Sometimes Frank wondered if Kevin had taken a map and actually pinpointed the place that would put the most distance between the two of them. Of course he'd never admit that. Kevin, like his mother, persisted in fables long past the point of comfort. His current favorite tale was the one about the two of them, how they were close, family. After Sheila's last hospitalization Frank had had to call Kevin. A horrible phone call that had ended with Kevin sobbing over Sheila, Frank putting the receiver quietly down. The boy had sent Frank letters, long anguished tomes Frank could hardly read. When Frank didn't answer, he'd slowed down to cards, followed by a subscription to the newspaper of the town the boy now called home. A place Kevin insisted was "God's country," as if God, Frank snorted to himself, was a credulous hick. Each week Frank was forced to pull a rolled copy of the *Salish Bay Recorder* from the pile of other supplications that filled his mailbox, undo its brown paper wrapper, and dump it unread into a box in the garage.

Old habits died hard: Frank carried the glass in a dustpan to the garage. Never, he had instructed Sheila and Kevin, throw out dangerous material in the house. Sheila ignored him. When Kevin was a child and would break a glass dish or porcelain cup (a not infrequent event), she would insist that each of them take one of the remaining pieces and smash it to the ground, making a silent wish at the same time. The act, according to Sheila, was supposed to transform bad luck into good, a sort of nose-thumbing toward the winds of fate.

As Frank struggled with the garbage can lid, a piece of glass shimmied from the dustpan to the concrete floor as if to prove his point. *See*, he wanted to say. And yet as he bent to sweep the glass back into the dustpan, Frank couldn't help noticing how the fragments of glass resembled territories on a map, divided by thick borderlines of open space, and he felt himself sinking, disappearing into that no man's land.

See, he heard his wife's voice say so clearly that he spun around, squinting past the old Buick for a glimpse of her crooked smile. As he turned, the toe of his slipper caught on a crack in the floor, and Frank fell headlong into an awkwardly stacked cardboard box, the same one that held eight months of *Salish Bay Recorder*s. Kevin's newspapers spilled with fervor; they shot out of their box and landed on Frank's chest. He swore extravagantly, his voice ricocheting off the concrete floor of the garage. He struggled to sit up, noticing as he did a front-page photograph on one of the newspapers: a group of heavily dressed, bearded men gathered around a large rock on an apparently windswept beach. The caption, set in large type, read:

Annual Winter Crabfest Lures Hermits.

It took Frank some time to realize that the word *hermits* referred not to the circle of unsmiling men but to the crabs simmering in the pot beside the beach rock. By the time he figured that out, he was nearly hooked. Who ate hermit crabs? He pulled a stack of papers from his lap and hobbled to the concrete step that led to the den, seated himself on the Astroturf mat, and spread the first of the newspapers out neatly on the floor. Smoothing the corners of the paper, he read a line here, a paragraph there. Soon, his sore foot forgotten, he was reading his way through months of newspapers, following scandals and debates, watching as, before his eyes, the charming hideaway that Kevin had found took shape. Tucked in among the articles on zoning and petty crime (soapsuds dumped in the courthouse fountain), he discovered the most astonishing headlines:

Chinese Treasure Found Behind Cannery

Burton Durkle Rescues Submerged Women

Entrepreneur Opens House of Memories

And the letters! Written in a language that Frank considered old-fashioned, these missives were both formal and rich in colloquialisms.

To the Esteemed Editor, one began. *Being a man of little education and much practical knowledge, I can only state that the information relayed in Mr. P. E. Thomlinson's letter of February 22nd was a lot of hooey and a darned shame. Roger Mulkey never did and never would steal seed from another man's oyster beds. I have known the man for years and he is upstanding. Do you not have anything better to do than print slanderous rubs against good folk? I suggest you enlarge the sports news. Simple minds can never get enough of football.*

After an hour or so, Frank put the papers down, pulled out his pen and notebook and sketched a rough map of Salish Bay, imagining a tidy stretch of downtown shops along the water, the single twisting road that led out of town, the neat squares of the uptown blocks with their streets named after minor statesmen. He carried the stack of *Recorder*s into the den and spent the night reading them, falling further and further in love with the small town whose inhabitants, in the grainy black-and-white photos that appeared sporadically throughout the paper, seemed both dignified and exotic.

Just as the sun was rising, somewhere deep in the October 16th issue, Frank was alarmed to find a two-paragraph article buried among the court notices and permit applications. The article described the plan of a developer, a man named Hudbury. This Hudbury was planning a resort right on the northern edge of town. The details of the development plan were sketchy, but the scope was clear to Frank. With a new marina, a mini-mall, a campground, two restaurants, and an underwater aquarium, Hudbury was proposing to change Salish Bay irrevocably. Frank closed his eyes and imagined trains of luxury sedans streaming into town driven by men sporting dark glasses and cellular phones, men who looked just like the young men who had shunted him into early retirement from the plant, all of them buying up Salish Bay without even coming to an idle.

Before Frank quite realized what he was doing, he was seated at the desk in the hallway writing a long, impassioned letter on his wife's blue stationery. He had carried the candied apple downstairs to a corner of Sheila's desk. Now he found himself staring into the apple and fabricating a persona. In order to increase his validity (no one, especially his son, would put much weight on *his* opinion) he pretended that he had grown up in Salish Bay. He added twenty-five years to his age, becoming, even as he wrote, a sage elder citizen exiled in the far foreign climes of the eastern sea board. *At my age,* he wrote, *I feel I have, not necessarily the right, but the perspective to address your dilemma.* He did all of this without giving much thought to his deceit. Perhaps a part of him did not believe, despite the evidence of the newspapers scattered across his den, that Salish Bay was real. Could there really be such a place where debates of the heart and discussions of good and evil were tied on a weekly basis to storm sewers and school bonds? He included his street address but omitted his phone number. Then he found Sheila's cache of stamps, and, still in his stocking feet, he hurried along the frozen path to the mailbox at the end of the driveway where he placed the letter, raising the red flag like a declaration of war.

You had to have an attitude. This had been Frank's theory on social interaction. Otherwise who could take you seriously? He had always imagined he projected a certain staunch intelligence, that anyone could look at him and see a man with a wealth of facts at his disposal, a man whose intellect prevailed over his emotions. Yet, since last summer when he retired from the plant, Frank had become less sure of himself. He'd tried an outing here and there. A few movies. A quick beer at the local tavern. Nothing felt right. He was besieged by incidents that told him he appeared as furtive as he felt. A theater manager asked him to change his seat after he inadvertently frightened two children by falling asleep beside them. Checkout girls—pudgy women with too much makeup and dyed hair—started arguments with him over the correct spelling of Quik-Chek or the value of Canadian pennies (of course they were worth *something,* Frank insisted).

The day after he wrote to the paper he decided to treat himself to a pastrami sandwich from Lynchburg's Deli. Although cold, the day was clear, the sky so blue it made Frank giddy. He would picnic beside the school playground across from his house. Kevin had attended the school in its halcyon days when both the school and the development that surrounded it were new. Frank couldn't count the number of evenings he had spent in that playground, instructing Kevin ceaselessly on the straight kick and bent release of swinging, while Sheila was out at one of her play rehearsals. The two of them, father and son, had spent more time in that playground than they had in their own backyard.

Frank stopped home just long enough to slip a bottle of Miller into his paper bag before striding toward the playground where he crouched on the end of the sliding board and spread his lunch over his lap with his gloved hands. He cracked open the beer, took a long swig, and put the bottle down on the gravel beside the slide, where it promptly fell over, soaking his pant leg in the process. He was just righting the bottle when a loud buzzer crashed through the air, causing his heart to leap painfully. In seconds the playground was rushed by a crowd of children who stopped short when they saw Frank sitting on the edge of the slide. A frightened-looking woman rushed back into the school, returning in what seemed like an instant with a bald-headed man close to Frank's own age, overdressed in a black overcoat like a funeral director. Frank was already rewrapping his sandwich in its white butcher paper, fumbling because of his gloves and the cold, when the man stopped a few feet in front of him.

"I'm sorry," Frank began, "I thought it was Saturday."

"Saturday," the man said in an astounded voice. "Saturday! It's Tuesday, fellow, Tuesday!" The woman reached out and grabbed two young boys heading for the slide's ladder and thrust them behind her.

Frank started to explain. "I'm retired—"

"Mister Von Draker!" Another even younger woman came rushing up breathlessly, stopping short beside the first woman. "Mister Von Draker, the police are on the way."

"Oh, come on," Frank sputtered again. "I live just across the street." He pointed, expecting all eyes to turn toward his wholesome split-level, but when he looked with them he was shocked to see a decrepit house with chipped siding and an overgrown lawn, a prominent window covered by a ragged piece of cardboard.

"I'll go home," he said. He pushed the sandwich back into the paper sack and began to shamble across the graveled playground.

"Ex*cuse* me," the man called out, and when Frank turned he pointed to the beer bottle lying beside the sliding board.

For two days Frank could not go out. He kept seeing the looks of repulsion and alarm on the faces of the principal and his staff. Over and over his heart clenched with humiliation as he heard again the great whoosh of silence when the children, flooding toward the playground, spotted him.

While going through the mail on his third day housebound, Frank noticed an advertisement for home delivery from a nearby market. The market was an older one he remembered from the early days in the neighborhood before the shopping centers had been built out on Route 202. The ad promised a wide inventory. Why, they could even supply motor oil and postage stamps. He made a list and telephoned. A half-hour later, without argument, he received his boxes of groceries from a pleasingly uncommunicative teenager.

Throughout that first housebound week, Frank almost managed to forget his impetuous letter. But on Tuesday he remembered and for the first time wondered if the editors of the *Recorder* would print the letter without the required phone number. He was frankly a little aghast at his own audacity. Wednesday, the paper's publishing day, came and went, and he was anguished with anticipation until he realized that *he* would have to wait for the cross-country mail to bring his copy. When, finally, on the following Friday the rolled parcel arrived, he was shocked to find that not only had the editors published his letter, but he was the featured letter writer, his nom de plume, Mr. Andrew Glenn, glistening in boldface type from the center of the page under the heading: *The Wisdom of Experience*. Frank's heart beat as mercilessly as if he had just entered the town naked on a horse.

A week later it was clear that Andrew Glenn had ignited a controversy of unforetold proportions. Frank, being a new subscriber, had not known about the condo project of five years ago, the one built on the site of the former grammar school at the top of Mariner's Hill. Wounds, never fully healed, were reopened as old-timers lamented the loss of their valuable playing fields. Even newcomers to Salish Bay rushed to raise questions. Frank wondered with a pang if Kevin had read his letter, if he too had jumped on the Andrew Glenn bandwagon, which was gathering supporters with alarming speed. Hudbury, it turned out, had been behind the condo project as well, but the price he paid the school district, outstanding though it seemed at the time, had turned out to be a pittance in comparison to the land's true value.

"And, now," wrote Pete Pilsmacher, the dentist and daredevil kayaker, "Hudbury wants our shoreline."

"Thank the lord," a matron named Marjorie Sather wrote, "for the sharp eyes of Andrew Glenn. His is the voice of old Salish Bay, one well worth attention."

Even the editor, Lovell Burdine (who, Frank was

sure, must have made the decision to bury Hudbury's plan in the paper's back pages), weighed in. "Perhaps," his editorial concluded, noting the fact that Andrew Glenn no longer abided in Salish Bay, "we can encourage Mr. Glenn to come home. Salish Bay clearly needs him and his obvious good sense."

But Hudbury was not so easily dissuaded. Even as opposition built, his plans continued. Suddenly visible, he plied the town with charts and maps, promises and bribes, study heaped upon study. City council meetings became impossible as they often had to be canceled and the crowds dispersed because the number of attendants swelled far beyond that permitted by the fire code.

Oh, but Hudbury was insistent. He had allies: state people, corporate bigwigs. Frank was forced to write more letters, using his engineering expertise to point out the flaws in Hudbury's aquarium blueprints. For instance, half of the proposed resort would lie next to a salt-water lagoon, an obvious risk.

Men are not alone in this world, Frank had Andrew write, paraphrasing something he had heard in one of Sheila's plays. *Imagine the plight of the migrating birds, a natural habitat vanished. Without the solace of our natural community, we are all diminished, threatened with spiritual oblivion. Who among us would choose to play God with so obvious a hand? Would you, Mr. Hudbury?*

Frank notified the Audubon Society and the Sierra Club, the Wetland Protectors and the True Friends of the Earth. Weeks went by and he placed daily long-distance calls to the Salish Bay library to check facts. The librarian, Betsy Cadwalder, initially reticent, turned out to be a staunch opponent of any sort of development, and she eagerly provided him with the basis for detailed rebuttals of Hudbury's environmental statements. Finally, in early April, five months after Frank's first letter, four months after a citizens' commission formed to investigate past Hudbury developments, Hudbury pulled the plug on the project.

The town celebrated like crazy. They adored Andrew Glenn. Letters swarmed into the *Recorder*'s office with his name on the envelopes, and Lovell Burdine embarked on a campaign of his own: a weekly column penned by the town's most favored son.

"You can write on any topic," Frank read from Burdine's letter, "in any way."

Frank had to chuckle a little at that, thinking once again of Kevin, who couldn't sit still no matter what subject Frank chose. But maybe Kevin would find Andrew Glenn more compelling. Burdine went on to say that the length too was up to him, although he did want to point out that Andrew's letters were nearly perfect in their word count. The suggested payment astonished Frank, who had always believed that the people who wrote for local newspapers did so as a sort of hobby. His wife had written skits for the local repertory company and never received a dime.

At first Frank refused politely, but Lovell Burdine wrote again. The two weeks when Frank, deep into his anti-Hudbury research, had not written letters, the paper had been besieged with calls from readers concerned about his welfare. Many wanted his home address, which Burdine declined to make public. Thank God, thought Frank, flushed with the thought of a knock on his door.

"You have," Burdine continued, "increased our circulation with just your letters. Think what a column would do. Think, too, what good you could do for your hometown." Then Lovell Burdine named a new fee, quite a bit higher than the first one.

Holding Burdine's letter in his hand, Frank stared out the window over his wild lawn and the overgrown garden where his wife's gaily striped tulips announced another ragged spring. Although he had not left the house except to sweep the mailbox clean each evening, Frank had not felt truly lonely until this moment. A breeze rippled through his tall grass revealing candy wrappers and glistening pop cans pushing up like foreign bulbs he himself had planted last fall and forgotten. At that moment the decay around him seemed overwhelming. Only the crisp type of Burdine's letter made his heart easy, the simple black letters that spelled out Andrew Glenn's name. At Sheila's desk—Andrew's desk—Frank picked up his pen.

I would be honored, Mr. Burdine, he penned on behalf of Andrew Glenn.

Afterward, feeling as dazed as if he had just agreed to go on stage, Frank drifted through the house, picking up the scraps of paper and empty ice cream bowls that marked his progress through the rooms. He straightened his bedroom, setting a pair of his wife's ridiculous shoes upright on the closet floor, folding a forgotten sweater, dusting the cosmetics on the bureau, some of which were so dried out that Frank tossed them into the wastebasket. He called the market and arranged for them to pick up a piece of glass from O'Donnell's Hardware next door. Later that afternoon he knelt in Kevin's room and replaced the cardboard with a square of glass so clear and perfect the room seemed to come alive with light. Downstairs he found his last chore: the apple, rotted in its hard shell, slowly becoming a part of Sheila's desk.

It wasn't long before one of Andrew Glenn's admirers managed to uncover his address.

Frank's first column for Lovell Burdine was a description of his first foray into cooking after his wife's death. On the afternoon he received his copy of the paper, a thick ivory-colored envelope, also with a Salish Bay return address, appeared in Frank's box addressed to Andrew Glenn in an unfamiliar hand. The letter's first sentence took his breath away, and what followed nearly knocked him over.

Dear Andrew, he read, *I am taking a chance on you.*

Yes, the letter continued, *I am hoping that you will remember me. You will, no doubt, have forgotten much about the everyday life of your childhood over the years. Even when I was only forty, I know I struggled to remember commonplace details from my twenties and thirties, and I'm sure you have experienced the same subtle disintegration. Our memories are flimsy things unable to bear the weight of so many years, and one might assume that at our advanced age—let us not kid ourselves, Andrew: we are old!—we should surely be bereft of our infantile selves. Still, if you are like me, perhaps you are finding your memories returning. Just this morning as I was sipping my coffee—instant, still, with a hefty tablespoon of Cremora—I had a very clear picture of our sixth grade classroom.*

Do you recall how each afternoon the sun would slide across Mrs. Renkler's desk in a band that widened until it spilled over all our desks, blinding our eyes as we struggled to follow Mrs. Renkler's maps, her convoluted discourse on the Peloponnesian Wars? You were the tallest boy in the class (although, if I remember correctly, one of the youngest), and she often handed you the window pole to catch the edge of the paper shades and pull their rounded cords down the long wide windows of the Franklin Avenue building which housed our school then. Always, there was that moment when you, a slender golden-haired boy of eleven, balanced above the new heat registers. The window pole in your hand could have been an Athenian lance at Amphipolis, and you, although fair-featured, always drew your mouth into a hard line like a young warrior, like brave Cleon murdered by the forces of Brasidas, who met his own doom during that fateful battle. Oh, how we all admired you then, Andrew! And how pleasing, after all these years, to see your name again and imagine you in your distant home thinking of your younger days here with us.

The letter was signed Charlotte Langhorne Fisk, the Langhorne underlined. Frank recognized none of the names. His wife had had a friend named Char, a brassy young woman who invariably played the tart or the villainess in the local theater productions, but she was not a bright woman and was incapable, Frank was sure, of such an elaborate hoax. If indeed this was a hoax. (But what else could it be? Andrew Glenn did not exist outside Frank's imagination, did he?) In any case, it was doubtful that young Char could compose a legible shopping list let alone an eloquent letter. This Charlotte went on to hope that Andrew Glenn would find the time to communicate with her, perhaps share a bit of his life in the years since she had known him. Was this a trap? Frank wondered. A plot by Hudbury to unmask him? If so, it was a cleverly rendered plan—too clever, Frank decided, to be a Hudbury ruse. This woman, and Frank wanted dearly to believe she was real, seemed anxious to have a compatriot in memory even as she apologized for what she called her ramblings. Frank found himself nodding to her words and, although he could not bring himself to answer her, he felt the warm, unfamiliar rush of companionship.

Frank devoted his second column to a spirited defense of Salish Bay's so-called street kids, a group of local youth who used the hill that wound down from Henry Clay Street to Stephen Douglas Avenue to set up a skateboard half-pipe. He had been impressed by the construction of the complex skate path, and he was oddly moved when the *Recorder* printed a photo of one

Jasper Krabill, fifteen years old, surfing the air, an expression of pure joy upon his face. *Where lies the richness of life*, Andrew wrote, *but within adventure, a pursuit of challenges and dangerous joys, a sudden rising out of our small selves, an expansion toward heaven?*

The Friday after his skateboard column, Frank received his copy of the paper accompanied by an uncashable check made out to Andrew Glenn from Lovell Burdine and another letter from Charlotte Fisk. Frank quickly put aside everything else and opened Charlotte's letter, which continued as if their conversation, if it could be called that, had been only momentarily interrupted.

It is silly, I think, to spend one's later years obsessed by the details of earlier times, but it must be the natural way of things. Otherwise, why would memories be so fascinating, so deeply compelling? Still, I know how they bore all but the direct participants, and I've been careful to keep my wanderings through yesterday in check. Most of my peers are gone. I am, as they say, sitting in the front row, but that does not preclude a backward glance now and then.

I won't lie to you, Andrew. Not all of my memories are pleasant. I was married as you may know to Scott Fisk. He worked with your cousin, Leonard, at the mill and they were, for some years, inseparable friends. Leonard, as I'm sure you know, had a difficult youth—no, let me stick to my resolve and be honest—Leonard was *a difficult youth and a more difficult man. He was, unlike the rest of your family, quarrelsome and mean-spirited, and my husband adored him.*

Scott Fisk, Leonard Glenn—of course Frank knew nothing of these men. A black-and-white photograph, a tiny white-bordered square, fell out of the envelope. Clothed in the suits and fedoras of Frank's early childhood, two young men caught by an unwelcome photographer were about to push open a frosted glass door with the words *Clark Tavern* etched on it. The taller man, his face partly shadowed, gazed directly into the camera with what seemed to be the suggestion of a sneer lifting the right—the lit—side of his face. His hands were half-raised at his side. Startled by the flash of the camera, he had pivoted neatly on the balls of his feet, ready to fight. There was a sharpness to his figure that struck Frank as vaguely familiar, as if the man were indeed a long-lost relative. The other man, open-faced and freckled, looked merely confused, his gaze riveted in worry upon the tall man's figure as if waiting for a cue. He was almost a boy and Frank recognized with a shock a striking resemblance to his own son, Kevin.

Maybe it was the photograph. The young man so like his son, his Kevin at home in Salish Bay. Frank did not mean to write back; in fact an hour later he was consumed by guilt, inwardly declaring his act to be a grievous deception, but at the time he could not stop himself. It was as if he was under a spell, Andrew's spell, one that compelled him to answer the courage of this unknown elderly woman, a woman for whom Frank felt unaccountably responsible. He intended to keep his letter short, a gentlemanly missive apologizing for his own bad memory, expressing gratitude for her kind words and misplaced admiration, but then he decided to add a few brief biographical notes in response to her queries.

My life, he wrote in all sincerity, *has been a quiet one made rich by the presence of my wife. She would have loved Salish Bay, and I regret that we never had the chance to visit together during her lifetime. I send you my own condolences on the death of Scott Fisk, who I remember as an open, trusting fellow. Although I was never close to my cousin, I feel sure that you are right about Leonard, and I am filled with remorse that my own kin should have caused you pain. I don't recall much of our lessons on the battle at Amphipolis, but I do remember the story of the Seven Sleepers of Ephesus. Was it Mrs. Renkler who told us their tale? Do you remember it? How seven young martyrs were sealed in a cave. Centuries later they awoke and left the cave to reassure the emperor of the presence of God. In truth I feel less like a young warrior at Amphipolis than like one of the Sleepers myself, stirring from the cave for a momentary appearance, then swiftly returning.*

Sheila had given him that story. Like thousands of others relayed over the dinner table or from the bathtub. Tales and fables: Sheila had been the mistress of them. He thought he had forgotten them all, and yet Charlotte's mention of the war between Athens and Sparta had brought at least this story back. Those two feuding city-states like sibling children: the one, brilliantly intuitive; the other, made strong through discipline and pain. Sheila favored Athens, added its fables to her storehouse.

Oh how it had bothered him when she spouted nonsense to Kevin. It hadn't been just the old saw about filling a child's head with nonsense. Frank already assumed that Kevin's head was full of prattle: the transforming bite of apple, the bewitched frog. He'd been such a gullible child, the kind of kid who really believed one could dig a hole in the backyard right to China or bring dead gerbils back to life by stating a categorical belief in fairies. Holidays had been misery for all of them, Sheila perpetuating myths well past a reasonable age.

"He needs to know the truth," Frank had insisted after spilling the beans on Santa Claus.

"Why?" Sheila had said, her face full of angry tears. "He's a six-year-old child."

"Exactly," Frank had countered.

As he folded his letter to Charlotte into its envelope, he marveled at his old ruthlessness. His mission to dislodge the pastel make-believe world in his son's mind and replace it with rock-solid facts now made him uneasy. Although nothing had seemed more right at the time, he itched with a desire to take back every word.

After the mailman came and lowered the red flag, Frank tried to forget about Charlotte, but Andrew's next column wrote itself: the tale of a weak-minded, good-hearted fellow led into thievery and accidental death by a smooth-talker. Andrew Glenn told it as a parable, leaving the moral unsaid. What was the moral? Frank didn't know, and he worried for a week that the town would think Andrew was drifting. "Having a senior moment," his wife would have called it. But he needn't have been concerned. Bob Chase, Salish Bay's mayor, would label the column "a brilliant commentary on the relationship between our small town and the hucksters who continually propose to steal its soul."

The next week, another letter from Charlotte:

I was working at the hospital then in the admittance office. My hours were long and mostly at night since Walter, our son, was not yet in school. When I was at work, Leonard came over to the house, and he and Scott would spend the evening polishing one of Leonard's scams, roughhousing with Walter until the little boy cried and fell asleep, then they'd leave him there curled in his damp bed and walk downtown to the tavern to play pool. Leonard and Scott were good-looking men and you can imagine how Salish Bay was in those days, just after the war, so many women alone, widows with war pensions or lonely wives with businesses they could not run alone. How vulnerable those women were! In retrospect such an accident as Leonard engineered was probably just a matter of time. People will do what they are meant to do, regardless of moral opposition.

Indeed, Frank concurred, they will. He suddenly remembered Sheila and Buckley Thomas, a man she'd known in her theater group, a long-suppressed image of the two of them, mere shadows in the back row of an empty theater on the one night Frank chose to attend rehearsal. How could Frank have forgotten the feeling he had when he finally focused on them, heads together, legs lifted onto the seats in front of them and intertwined? And later Sheila, laughing at him, saying it was all part of the rehearsal. See, she'd said, giving him her lopsided grin, even you can fall for the magic of make-believe. Of course, of course. Which didn't explain a kiss Frank also thought he saw after the final performance.

Oh, Frank, Sheila had sighed. *Please.*

She'd fallen crooning into his arms, as if she were trying to soften his hard heart. In reality he held her easily, wanting her desperately, his heart dancing with confusion.

They never mentioned the kiss.

And his son—gone, gone, gone with nary a backward glance. In a phone conversation shortly after he left school, Kevin had blurted out that he could not imagine living a life like Frank's. "I don't have those kind of goals, Pop," he said as if Frank had suggested he take up bank robbery. "It's not what I'm meant for."

Later that evening, rereading Charlotte's letter, Frank imagined Andrew Glenn arriving back in town just in time to grab his cousin Leonard by the scruff of the neck and knock some sense into him and save Scott Fisk. Perhaps Charlotte had made desperate attempts to locate Andrew. Maybe she blamed him still for all he'd left undone when he said goodbye to Salish Bay. Oddly, when Frank thought of Charlotte he pictured her not as the elderly woman she must be, but as Sheila one trying night during Kevin's horrible thirteenth year. One of those sudden, unavoidable fights had sprung up between Frank and the boy. It had started with something small, a sneer that sent a wave of fury over Frank who had already sat up an hour past his bedtime waiting for the kid to come home. Words surged into shouts, his hand was raised to strike even as the boy slammed out of the house.

"Go after him," Sheila commanded from the stairs where she witnessed the finale.

She'd been dressed for bed when the fight started, a pink kimono thrown carelessly over her nightgown. Makeup off, her eyes tired but bright with emotion, she seemed less a wife than an unforeseen and powerful voice of reason, and Frank had obeyed, cursing as he cruised in the Buick until he spotted Kevin blocks away, heading resolutely toward the highway. Only now did Frank realize what a child the boy had been and how close they had come to losing him then. But for Sheila he would have let the boy go, daring him to be the man he pretended to be. Yes, that was how he envisioned Charlotte: a much older, steadier Sheila, a pink kimono sheathing her elderly body as she composed letters to a childhood friend.

In her next letter Charlotte enclosed a fist-sized package with bits of pale blue glass from a beach she was sure he would remember—Baker's Beach. *The beach you saved,* she prompted, *Hudbury's target.* Also in the package was a class ring from Salish Bay High School, the initials SF carved beneath the dark, apple-red garnet. For a moment Frank wondered why Charlotte parted with the ring, but, when he glanced up to see the pieces of beach glass glowing in the dulled candy dish where he had placed them, Frank knew.

Sheila had *taken* everything, he realized, when she left. The color, the light, the subtle nuances of taste—all gone. "Oh, Mom," the boy had sobbed, and Frank had tucked the receiver back in its cradle. In contrast Scott Fisk and Leonard Glenn had suffused Charlotte's life with pain. Of course she wanted to rid herself of any physical connection to that past. While Frank's house was a hollow cave, hers throbbed, years and years after the mysterious event to which Charlotte still referred as "the accident," with her husband's presence. Should he ask her more? Would Andrew?

Dear Charlotte, I do not wish to intrude on painful memories, and clearly there is nothing I can do now to stave off the horrific events of the past, but I wonder greatly what wrong has been done.

No, he couldn't write such a thing. A voyeur, that's what he sounded like. But even as he posited his question to Charlotte, he became aware of another set of questions lingering behind him as if Charlotte, grasping his hand and entering his life, now was glancing around his own forlorn home, her easy old face crumbling with a disappointment she struggled to hide. Her still brilliant eyes turned on him as she took in his hermit's nest of a den, the stacks of delivery boxes waiting on the back stoop, all the hallmarks of his untended life: *Was this what you wanted?*

Ephesus, Charlotte continued in her next letter, *was one of Mrs. Renkler's favorite subjects. And the Seven Sleepers—yes, I remember the story well, and I will allow your self-comparison. In fact, since you mentioned it, I can't help thinking of Andrew Glenn as the Eighth Sleeper of Ephesus, putting his weary shoulder to the boulder beside the cave's opening simply for the sake of restoring a stranger's faith. (The emperor's name, by the way, was Theodosius II.)*

Ephesus. Oh, Mrs. Renkler was devoted to the subject! The quizzes to which she subjected us—Andrew, how could you not recall those? A town of unspeakable wealth, Ephesus contained one of the Seven Wonders of the World, the Temple of Diana, did it not? Rich Croesus and Alexander the Great, even the Romans, all possessed the city in their turn. The Ephesian slave market was reputedly the largest in the world. And, of course, the city was eventually destroyed by the greed and avarice of its inhabitants who tempted the rampaging Goths.

That night they took Walter with them. It was Leonard's idea, I'm sure, but Scott did not resist. What kind of a father, you may ask, would risk the loss of his own son? Perhaps he thought a young child, his face soft with sleep, would charm anyone, no matter how hot her temper. Shots were fired. Accidentally, it was claimed. After all, the gun was Leonard's. Does it matter now whose fingers struggled for the gun?

Oh, Andrew, the Goths. Do they ever rest from their burrowing rampages? What great havoc has been raised by marauders who claim no place as their home and everywhere as possession! And how brave the Seven Sleepers must have been to step from their sheltered cave, across the threshold of imagined time, just to ease another soul's path.

Perhaps I should I say this more clearly: God bless you, Andrew.

Yes, Frank thought, as he refolded the letter gently and placed it in Sheila's desk drawer, God bless you, Andrew, whoever you are.

Despite the chattering of crickets, the surflike sound of traffic on nearby Route 202, Frank was suffused with a sudden peace. He lay in bed, the breeze ruffling the sheet over him, and dreamed that people were assembling outside on the street. They garlanded his house while, across the way beside the jungle gym, the schoolchildren gawked. Their principal, the officious Mr. Von Draker, pushed forward, only to be compelled to retreat as the crowd rippled toward Frank's door. Frank thought he heard his wife call out his name, and he swung open his front door to embrace, not Sheila, who a year ago he'd missed with a grief so intense he felt his own life slipping away, but the whole of Salish Bay. Frank recognized them all from their photos in *The Recorder*. There was Lovell Burdine beside Mayor Bob Chase, the council member Marilyn Littleton and Gaylord Cox, the cannery owner, a score of downtown kids including Jasper Krabill who flipped his skateboard into the air and gave him the whassup sign. Over on the edge of the crowd, a young woman, her dark hair braided neatly down her back, her strong-looking arms piled with books, a sweet, intent expression on her face: Betsy Cadwalder, his librarian. In the midst of the crowd, dead center in the front row, one small still figure caught his eye, a white-haired woman whose head barely reached young Jasper's elbow. She beamed at Frank and held out her hands, and, for the first time in nearly nine months, Frank left the boundary of his yard and stepped out into the world, looking for one more familiar face.

One Friday, as suddenly and mysteriously as they'd begun, Charlotte's letters ceased. Frank fretted through an entire week before he decided that he must call Lovell Burdine. Silly of him not to realize it earlier, but it must have been Burdine who had given her his address. Who else? He found the paper's phone number in a back issue and was stunned to hear how quickly he was connected to Salish Bay. A secretary took his call and put him on hold.

"Burdine," a voice barked.

"Lovell Burdine?" Frank inquired weakly.

"Speaking," the man said. Immediately Burdine covered the mouthpiece slightly and shouted, "Not there!" at someone in his office.

"Okay," he said into the phone, "go ahead."

"Mr. Burdine," Frank took a breath and said it, his voice trembling slightly, "this is Andrew Glenn."

Oh, you might have thought Jesus Christ was on the line, Frank thought, amazed by the immediate reverential politeness that resulted. Standing in his kitchen, he caught sight of himself reflected in the wall oven, a concave image of a middle-aged man, and could not help thinking of Charlotte's golden-haired classmate, the white knight who fled town.

"That was a hell of an article about divorce, Andrew," Burdine began. "The letters haven't stopped."

"Well, thank you, but—"

"And the one about holding your kid—I can hear the typesetters weeping in the back room even now." A buzzer sounded somewhere in the background, and Burdine paused. Quickly Frank asked him about Charlotte.

"Old Charlotte Fisk?" Burdine pondered. "No, Andrew, I don't know her personally. Of course I saw her during that Hudbury fiasco, but she wouldn't talk to me. You say you're old friends?" Burdine seemed amazed at this information.

Frank hesitated before saying, "Yes, old, dear friends. We've been . . . uh, corresponding."

"You have?" Burdine was incredulous. "All through the Hudbury thing?"

"Well, no, afterwards." Frank was sweating. "Why," he stuttered to Burdine, "why do you sound so shocked?"

"Well, hell, Andrew," Burdine said, "I'm just wondering how you two could be so chummy when she was trying to sell all her land to Hudbury, and you were doing your damnedest to stop the deal."

"Her land?"

"C'mon, Andrew, you didn't know the Point belonged to old Mrs. Fisk?" When Frank didn't answer, Burdine continued, his voice thick with confidentiality. "Listen, Andrew, old man, I don't want to mess between two old friends, but if I'd known, I'd have advised you to steer clear. Charlotte Fisk has a reputation around here, going way, way back to her husband's accident in the forties. Some people say," he laughed uneasily, "that she is a . . . well, a witch. The conjuring kind, if you know what I mean. But, listen, I'll find out what I can. She's got some help now, a college kid nurse. I'll have him get back to you. Give me your number again."

Frank's heart shifted. "It's long distance, of course," he stalled.

"No problem," Burdine countered, waiting until Frank slowly began to recite the digits that would link him to Andrew Glenn.

Although he used his phone several times a week to arrange deliveries or call Betsy Cadwalder at the library for specific information, Frank seldom received calls. The unaccustomed ringing never failed to pierce his chest and make his heart thump wildly, and he let the telemarketers or pollsters or wrong numbers ring their way to exhaustion. Late at night on the evening of his talk with Lovell Burdine, Frank woke out of a dream where his wife was tugging on his sleeve urging him to join her in some silly game and, out of a long forgotten reflex, grabbed the phone on its second ring.

"Pop," he heard when he gingerly lifted the receiver to his ear. "Pop, you there?"

"Kevin," Frank said. He wasn't sure he wasn't still dreaming. Still he was surprised at how relieved he felt to hear his son's voice.

"Pop. It *is* you. I've been trying to reach you forever," Kevin said. "You're a busy guy."

"Actually, I retired," Frank said. "Over a year ago now."

"I know that." A little of the old exasperation crept into Kevin's voice but faded into perplexity as the boy continued. "Tried to call you at Christmas too," he said. "You sent me presents."

Frank switched on the night-table lamp and sat up. "Where are you, Kevin?"

"Home. I'm home."

"Here?"

"No, no," his son laughed, as if anyone could mistake Frank's house for a home. "I'm in Salish Bay."

Frank felt a sudden flush as he readied himself to explain. It began with an apple, he wanted to say. No, wait . . . a newspaper, its old-fashioned narrow columns listing eastward like a line of ancient, unsteady buildings crumbling into waterfront. Perhaps only Frank could see clearly the figure of a middle-age man, both foreigner and native son, emerging onto that unfamiliar shore, one hand extended in shy greeting. The image floated toward Frank as surely as if he were on the bay himself, caught between the neglected façades and their quavering reflections.

"Pop, you there?" Kevin's sweet concern caught Frank, pulled him steady.

"Of course," he managed to whisper, "of course, honey. I'm here now."

ACQUIESCENCE

EVELYN HATCH HAD NEVER THOUGHT OF HERSELF AS THE kind of person who could become a stalker. Her childhood, although dreamy and inward, possessed none of the thwarted desires, the unrelenting misery, that were, she imagined, heralds of disturbances to come. She'd been shy as a child, willful as a teen, narcissistic as a young woman—altogether normal. Granted, she had gone through a period of excessive physical confidence, casting off admirers with a latent ruthlessness that she found more than vaguely pleasurable (one young man, a geology student, followed Evelyn for days after his rejection, leaving cairns of quartz, common basalt, and striated limestone on her doorstep to mark his presence), but she'd also been unsettled by her power and relieved when her first serious boyfriend, the one she loved, proposed, and she could ease off stage.

In middle age Evelyn Hatch, now Evelyn Rondeau,

retained an aura of calm grace, despite three children and an engineer husband who traveled often for business, leaving her alone for weeks at a time to deal with the daily crises of parenting. She put in long hours as an editor of an obscure journal devoted to ornamental gardening, and all her free time was spent supervising the children, the youngest of whom, a girl nine years old, was entering that sulky era her two older children, boys fifteen and sixteen, were just casting off. It was necessary for Evelyn to be available every evening if just to be the island around which those three tides ebbed and flowed and continually crashed. As a result, every six weeks or so, she succumbed to a cold or a sick headache that required her to spend an entire Sunday in bed while her husband trundled their daughter to visit his parents and the two teenagers came and went in loud whispers along the upstairs hallway. The oldest one was driving (a celery green Dodge Dart that had belonged to Evelyn's brother, Jimbo, a make-out artist of the first degree during his own high-school years), and his car often idled in the driveway with the radio blaring hard-edged remakes of pop songs Evelyn had known as a teenager.

Hers did not seem a bad life. The kids were healthy; she was frequently complimented; she had a fine perennial garden that bloomed continually and a husband who seemed genuinely to love her. All the great horrors of modern life had so far passed her by. If her husband drank too much at parties, if he sometimes failed in sensitivity, she forgave him easily. After all, Evelyn wasn't always the tender wife; she had her hard wild side. Once she had deliberately thrown a dozen eggs, one by one, at her husband during an argument over where they would celebrate the holidays—her family's house or his, where the holiday tradition included sententious speeches and frightened, stiff-necked children who performed as if radio-controlled by her even stiffer father-in-law. She could recall with a satisfied chagrin how her husband ducked and swayed, his mouth opening in astonishment each time an egg struck his body.

"Are you *insane?*" he had shrieked as he grabbed her by the wrists.

Yet Evelyn believed she was devoted to him. She never offered a second glance to another man in their suburban village. The better looking ones were so obviously on the make that they conjured up the word *disease* in her mind; the rest, husbands of her friends, were like an extended group of brothers. She hugged them goodnight after parties and felt only relief when she pulled away. None of them appealed to her half as much as her own husband did. She thought she would grow old gracefully, join do-gooder clubs, and look forward to grandchildren.

Maxwell Tranter had moved to town a year ago last fall. Evelyn couldn't remember the first time she glimpsed him, perhaps at one of her daughter's soccer games. He was a cello player, famous apparently, but his name was not familiar to her. Maxwell performed with the symphony and commuted into the city several days a week. The dentist's wife had heard him interviewed on the radio several years ago. His wife, Claudie, taught computer programming in the retraining program for displaced loggers and fishermen. They had one child, a boy, Adam, who attended the same alternative school as Evelyn's daughter. A friend of Evelyn's husband introduced her to Maxwell formally at a potluck, but by that time she'd already noticed him coming and going throughout town, wandering through the food co-op, racing his mountain bike along the river path where she sometimes ran. A tall, boyish man with graying hair. He often wore hooded sweatshirts like a teenage basketball player, and he drove a distinctive automobile—a red Alfa GTV. Evelyn kidded him about the car during that first meeting.

"A midlife crisis?" she'd said, raising one eyebrow.

Other men she knew would have rationalized the car or else made a crude joke designed to shock her.

"Obvious, isn't it?" he sighed. "Like a toddler trailing a blanket."

He had brilliant eyes, the pupils so large they appeared dilated. He questioned her intently about her work. None of the other local men ever did that. Not just *What do you do?*, but *Do you enjoy your work?* The dentist interrupted them, told a joke that neither found particularly funny. Evelyn smiled anyway. In fact she could not stop grinning broadly like a simpleton and felt, for the first time in a long while, ridiculously gawky. Maxwell's wife was younger and looked a bit like Evelyn, although Claudie's features were sharper, and she dressed more conservatively in dark blues and grays, a single touch of gold jewelry. We're of a type, Evelyn thought, and that made her glad. Glad to imagine that she might appeal to him. Later that evening she examined him again from across the living room. As if acknowledging her scrutiny he suddenly lifted his head and sent her his own appraising glance, weighted with a thick edge of clear desire. The air around her seemed laden with fine needles, and she panicked and found her husband. At the far end of the house she leaned on her husband's arm and flirted with him, rubbing one finger slowly up and down the inside of his thigh as they sat at the kitchen table, talking about summer vacations with a teacher from the alternative school and her officious boyfriend. They went home early, put the little girl to bed, and made silent frantic love behind their locked door.

She dreamed that night of the cello player, of his hand brushing her hair, a warm, seductive gesture. Even in the dream she felt her sleeping breath begin to pant. Her chest slowly contracted as if she were being crushed beneath him. In the morning she delivered her daughter to school and drove a roundabout way to work just so she could pass his house, a stucco cottage with a nondescript yard full of standard rhodies smothered in wood chips, the Alfa in the drive like a bright toy.

Later that afternoon she recognized Claudie Tranter

in the market. Claudie was shopping without a cart, like a man, choosing expensive brands of ordinary food. After following the cellist's wife furtively through several aisles, rolling her empty basket ahead of her, Evelyn became so agitated she had to leave the store.

I don't even know him, she cried to herself.

That night she dreamed again. This time they began by huddling together in his little car in the corner of a parking lot beside the river campground. His face swooped close, his mouth easing into hers. She could not recall a more intimate gesture and again woke up grieving.

For weeks this went on. Maxwell's house was on a steep hill, and more than once as the winter progressed, she fishtailed on black ice as she navigated her new detour to work. In February she put so many miles on the car that her husband noticed when he returned from one of his jobs.

"Evelyn?" he asked, half joking, "have you taken a road trip since I've been gone?"

She shrugged and laughed with him but began drinking rich, sluggish wines in the evenings to calm her rogue heart.

Once or twice—by accident, not her design—they ran into each other and conversed superficially like old friends, chitchat about nothing. A typical exchange, like the time her daughter and his son had gone to see a play with their school. The vans bringing them home from the city were late, and, like her, Maxwell avoided the growing queue of parents by the school doors, choosing instead to lean against the brick wall beside the playing fields, observing a flock of starlings twist and turn, corkscrewing across the sky in ever-changing formation. Five minutes they spoke, maybe less, and all the time he was rationalizing the children's delay by describing city traffic and lengthy curtain calls, she had wanted to scream out her desire, remind him of the passion of their dreamtime life. Instead she nodded and stammered gentle agreement. Their conversation was more banal than ever—classroom gossip—but again he leaned toward her with unusual interest. At one point, rattled by his attention, she dropped her car keys and he retrieved them. Placing them carefully in her hand, he let his fingers linger in her palm as if he were distracted by the traffic turning toward the school.

When the vans arrived she said goodbye to him hurriedly even though several minutes passed before the children and their teacher, laden with backpacks, playbills, and half-empty giant-size packages of theater licorice, disembarked from the vans. He lounged nearby the entire time, his long-fingered cellist hands almost touching her own. Later that evening, rushing around her kitchen, she slowly grew aware that she smelled different, that she was giving off the troubled odor of ripe, unpicked fruit.

Crazy, crazy, crazy. Each night she wondered how she kept going—correcting manuscripts, packing lunches, haggling with the older boys over chores, the girl over her impossible clothes, while all the time she was consumed with the inner saga of her love affair with Maxwell. Many nights, her husband away, the boys carousing, Evelyn and the girl watched videos, romantic comedies that set her to weeping in the dark of the den. A few times, readying her spring garden, she buried her face in the leaves of sage and English lavender and came up swamped in tears. Her oldest son caught her once, gazing off into space, her eyes hot. Allergies, she told him, what else? When her daughter was turning ten and making out the guest list for her birthday party, she wrote down the boy Adam's name, sending a thrill through Evelyn. The next night the girl crossed his name out, called him a jerk. He'd stolen a ball from her at recess. Evelyn marveled: How easily she let him go!

For a few days at a time she could forget him. Then she would be broadsided by another dream or the sight of him chatting with his son's teacher, the well endowed Ms. Sandy Allinka, in the school hall, and begin again, cruising like a teenager past the cottage on her way home from work, idling in the parking lot of the sporting goods store while he bought sneakers for his son. Once she even followed him into the dentist's office and leafed through one magazine after another, seeing nothing, reading nothing, flushing unaccountably when an inner door opened and the sound of the drill working on his teeth pierced the waiting room.

Then one Friday afternoon, on her way home

from work, Evelyn stopped at the liquor store to buy her weekend bottles of Merlot and Petite Syrah and noticed Claudie Tranter hauling empty cartons out to her car, a flashy silver and black four-wheel-drive vehicle, the kind Evelyn's sons called an "Amazon Coach." Were they moving? How could she ask? The woman didn't know her at all.

Evelyn went fishing, asked first her daughter: *Is Adam moving?* Her daughter, with grand indifference, shrugged and went back to braiding a hemp bracelet, one of dozens she would tie on her bird-boned wrist. Evelyn called the friend who'd introduced them at the potluck, fabricating a too long, too involved story about an old acquaintance relocating to town, wanting a cottage just like the one where the cello player lived with his wife. No, the friend said, I don't know of any. But later in the week the fish came swimming to the hook. Outside the garden center, the friend mentioned offhand, *I think they're getting divorced*.

Was this joy or was it grief? In high school she had known a boy who had to wash his hands every ten minutes, lathering each finger, scrubbing his palms until they were raw. Her college roommate pasted endangered animal stickers on their door and rubbed each one according to a particular order each time she left the room, even if she was just going down the hall to the lavatory. These regimens had seemed pitiable at first, but who could not see what satisfaction, what absolute contentment, resulted from obsession? Once they performed their tasks, the boy and her roommate were, however briefly, free from doubt and despair.

One late April morning, after her children had gone to school, her husband in Chile running structural checks of a new factory, Evelyn returned to her house and called in sick.

"But, Evelyn," her assistant whispered, hinting their boss was in the room, "your deadline."

"It can't be helped," she said, which was true. She had a terrific headache, she gasped into the phone, substituting heartache for headache in her mind.

Her older son's girlfriend had driven both boys to school, so she took the Dodge Dart as disguise. She donned a large, pale blue knit beret, sunglasses—the whole bit. The sky was a turbulent swirl of gray. Wisps of clouds rubbed their bellies along the meadow outside of town. His car was alone in the drive, a single light burning in an upstairs window. Gradually the sun emerged. A quick breeze opened the clouds and shook the day free. Evelyn should have been busy on the final copyedit of a piece about the architecture of fall bulbs, the miracle of their annual resurrection, but instead she trailed Maxwell first to the Lazy Susan Cafe for takeout coffee and the weekly *Recorder* and then to the river where he eased the Alfa beside the sign for the interpretive trails, set his coffee on the dashboard, and leaned back to read the paper.

She was not surprised that they'd ended up here. So many nights she'd dreamed this encounter. Still, she kept her distance. She passed the parking lot and took the next entrance, the one for the campground directly across the river. The campground was empty. She pulled into a spot beside a leaf-strewn picnic table. For five minutes she waited, hidden under trees. She could easily spend the day like this, she realized, the week, the next month—lose herself entirely in this haunting. Already her daughter had complained about the convoluted routes her mother took on the way to the market, the eye doctor, the library. Evelyn had to concoct elaborate lies about scouting for secret gardens, feeling each time a piece of what she still thought of as her soul crumble in despair.

As if accompanied by a wiser, older friend, she distinctly heard a voice, at first gently admonishing her, then pleading and cursing, but no hand was raised to hold her back when she opened the car door and slunk into the shadow of the cedars that darkened the river campground. Overcome by a sense of purpose, she wanted to believe the real heart of her had been here all along, waiting for him. Perhaps she knew him in another life and had now regained him like an ancient traveler who slips into a lost hollow by mischance and discovers Home in the virginal moss, the widening coolness of roots lying intertwined on the blind dirt. A light rain misted her face, yet Evelyn cast off the beret and sunglasses, ready to declare herself.

From her runs here in the summertime, Evelyn knew there was a rustic footbridge that crossed the river between the campground and the main parking lot where Maxwell waited. She found the trail easily. Winter blown branches lay between puddles. Banana slugs dotted the few patches of accessible trail. The air reeked of damp moss. Her shoes, silly felt clogs, were ruined in seconds, and her cotton socks squelched with damp. Evelyn ignored the voice that had started up again, imploring her to read each obstacle as a sign of misjudgment. Once she was in the middle of the bridge, she would appear as if floating in midair. He would come to her then, his secret lover, and touch her arm, admire with her the rocky eddies, the sudden sheen and easy collapse of water over rocks—a stunning acquiescence.

But two steps onto the narrow footbridge and Evelyn knew real trouble. The fir planks were so slick that one of her legs shot forward. A clog tumbled off and skated ahead of her to the middle of the bridge. She nearly skidded into the river, which, though only a short distance away, was swollen with spring rains. She landed hard on her knees. Arms flailing she finally managed to grasp the structure's meager log railing, feeling a long splinter enter her right palm just as the squeal of a fan belt announced the arrival of another car.

A moment later a van door slid open, releasing a racket of children's voices. A woman sung out for order, then his voice emerged. *His* voice! Shouting. *At her?*

The footbridge, Evelyn saw now, was screened from the parking lot's view by a thatch of snowberries. She had to crane her neck to see Maxwell ushering a group of children toward the interpretive trail on the far side of the parking lot. She recognized her own daughter's coat, a red plaid jacket that had once belonged to the older brother, so large it dwarfed the delicate girl. Evelyn watched as the school group swarmed, her daughter dancing blithely ahead of the cello player. Then, as the last child disappeared down the trail, she saw Maxwell pull back and swing one arm familiarly over the shoulder of the teacher, Sandy Allinka, who paused for one incredible second to rest her blond head on his shoulder.

For a moment Evelyn could not breathe. Her eyes half closed. The world spun.

She clutched the railing to steady herself, and the splinter in her palm responded with a sharp, fierce pain.

In the woods below, Maxwell and Sandy Allinka, their fingers laced together, followed the children toward a nurse log, the first marker on their forest tour.

"Look here," he called, and he bowed toward the ground to show Evelyn's daughter how the forest feeds upon itself, each seedling nourished in decay.

THE KING OF LIMBO

HIS PARTY IS OVER. HIS GUESTS HAVE GONE. HIS MOTHER is crying quietly in the bathroom. And William, now six years old, has left the tight nest of his bed to play with his new set of knights.

His mother gave him the knights to go with the castle his father made last Christmas. The castle, an elaborate wood and stucco construction, was the last project Greg made in the workshop in William's backyard. Now Greg has a new workshop in the cluttered garage of the woman he lives with in East Litchfield. Greg's girlfriend, Laurel, has twin sons two years older than William—Benny and Keith—and William knows his father has let them use the miniature hammer, saw, and chisels he used to keep in the workshop for him. William has seen the twins' feeble creations, balsa wood AK-47s splintered down one side. *Their* father is a doctor who lives in Colorado now with *his* new family. The father from that family has probably taken over yet another family, and so on. William lines up his foot soldiers, taps the foremost one, and the line snakes and falls like dominoes or fathers moving on.

Some of the new knights came on horses, and William has discovered that, if he pulls at just the right angle, he can pop a knight off his horse and move him still straddle-legged through the portcullis and into his castle. He hears a noise from beyond his closed door, the far-off hoofbeats of the opposing army. Goodwood, his parents' old Cairn terrier, is wheezing in the hallway.

Goodwood is dying, his mother says. He keeps dragging his decrepit body, covered with lumps and bald patches, down the stairs, out of the house, and under the oak tree in the side yard. And William's mother, equally stubborn, carries Goodwood back in, depositing him in the carpeted dog bed in the air-conditioned hallway. His mother believes that Goodwood should die here on the green shag remnants instead of in the heat of a July day borne up by the sharp upraised roots of the old oak. William is in the midst of storming the castle when he hears, beyond the dog's labored breathing, the opening of the bathroom door. He drops the knight, snagging his sword in the iron grate of the portcullis, and throws himself face down on the bed just as Scotty, his mother, opens his door.

She picks her way through the minefield of small toys that litter his floor and sits down beside him, leaning back against the headboard of his bed. William finds his body rolling into hers, but he wills himself still and keeps his eyes scrunched shut.

"It was a good birthday," she says rubbing William's back, circle over circle. "And not over yet. Tomorrow we'll go see the King of Limbo. The sun will shine, and Goodwood will wake us up barking, *It's William's birthday again!*"

William opens his eyes. He wants to tell her that Goodwood hasn't barked in days, and that he has already had too much birthday, but her reddened eyes and wavering voice stop him. He pretends he has been stunned by a blow from an enemy's broadsword. His open eyes stare across his pillowcase to the cobblestone fragments of his castle's forecourt. How will he ever earn his spurs if he keeps getting trounced by enemy knights?

"I'd like to invite Natife and Mr. Kennedy to come with us if you don't mind," his mother says. "You liked them, didn't you?"

William doesn't answer, but a ray of hope pierces the opening in his visor.

"Well, it's up to you, honey. We don't have to invite them if you don't want to."

Everything these days, it seems, is up to William. It makes him angry. The second time his father came to pick him up for his week at Laurel's, William had balked. His mother had half stripped his room, dividing up Legos, books, and cars. She had even started to put half his metal foot soldiers into a zip-lock bag. He had torn it from her hand and crawled under his bed. When his father arrived, William had refused to come out.

"It's okay," his father had said. He put his face down to talk to William, his new mustache picking up strands of lint and dog hair. "It's up to you, William."

That's what he said, but when William emerged a few minutes later it had been too late. His mother was alone in the kitchen, throwing cups of flour into a bowl as if she meant to make a mess, and only a circle of oil in the driveway marked the spot where Greg's car had sat impatiently.

As for the Nigerian, Natife, and his mother's colleague at the Chalwright School, Bernie Kennedy—William likes them. Especially the tall black man, Natife. He once gave William two white fluffy feathers he said came from a chicken. The feathers are exuberant things. William uses them as plumes in his aluminum foil helmet.

"Not like any chicken I've ever seen," Laurel had remarked.

But Scotty was pleased by Natife's gift to him, William knew. One of the many extra tasks she took on with her job as a humanities teacher at the Chalwright School was entertaining the newly arrived foreign students. Before his father left, William's family had hosted barbecues for Swedes, Christmas cookie parties for Brazilians, and a Halloween spookhouse where William saw a Greek girl plunge her head completely underwater to snag an apple. It's not often that a foreign student shows any genuine interest in William.

Scotty takes her hand abruptly from his back, and William is relieved. Sometimes his mother doesn't know when to stop. She clicks off the lamp attached to his headboard and is almost out the door before he manages to say: "Mom? It's okay if they come."

During the night Goodwood gives a tortured yelp that wakes William who leaves his bed and finds the dog midway down the stairs. William struggles with the dog and manages to pick him up like a baby, his front paws around William's neck. The dog smells like what William imagines a battlefield would: yellow pus draining from a wound, a poultice of bitter herbs, burning hair. He buries his face in the dog's fur. Death, William imagines, must be spicy.

In the morning Natife and Mr. Kennedy are waiting for them under the front portico of the Chalwright School. The Chalwright School occupies the grounds of a former estate with the white-pillared Federal-style mansion serving as the main school building. Although it rained earlier that morning, the day has already descended into a heated sheen of sunlight that brings out a lushness in the foliage surrounding the school. Bernie Kennedy presents Scotty with a fuchsia-colored azalea blossom that the rainstorm broke from an unsheltered bush in the center garden.

William doesn't know what to make of Bernie Kennedy. He tells stories about fierce animals and beautiful women. He lulls William into listening even when William doesn't understand what he is saying.

William likes the way Bernie's long-boned hands open like a surprised face or drift through the air, a powerful bird high on the wind. Sometimes he grabs William's ungiving body and swings him around until he grows loose and giggly. But mostly Bernie keeps his attention on Scotty. He admires her waist-length honey-brown hair, her wide hips. He stares openly at her behind whenever she moves away from him. Now he sits so close to her in the front seat of the old Volvo that Scotty has to say excuse me each time she shifts gears. The car is full of his chatter and her apologies.

William sits next to Natife in the backseat. He is belted, buckled, and snapped into his booster seat. The car could roll off a cliff and William would not budge. And he would have a great view. From the height of his car seat he can almost look Natife in the eye. Natife is not a talker. He plays little hand-slapping games with William, conveying the next move with an upraised eyebrow or a pointed finger. William likes to look at his hair. It runs in furrowed rows like the farm fields in William's picture books.

They are driving to Oak Hollow Park to watch the King of Limbo perform. It is one of William's presents from his mother. He saw the poster on a store window and recognized the word *King.* He has never seen a real king before.

A small crowd has already filled the folding chairs set up before the makeshift stage. The stage is at the rise of a gently sloping hill. From the top of the bleachers where they find seats, they can look down to Moon Lake. On the stage, men in loose fitting, brightly patterned shirts are setting up steel drums and microphones. The men begin hounding sound from the big steel drums. The bleachers tremble as people dance in their seats. William thinks the drums are like the summons of a horn echoing through a dark forest. He can't wait to see the king who will answer such a call.

A tiny brown man dressed in a thin silver costume walks onto the stage with two long wooden poles. He sets the poles into rubbery-looking cones and leaps back offstage, returning with a third pole. While he connects each end of the new pole to one of the upright ones, Scotty nudges William.

"There he is," she says.

"Where?" William's eyes search the stage. Two beautifully costumed women, visions of bright orange and pink with swirling gold rickrack, swish up in front of the drummers.

"Where?" William asks again.

"The little silver man. There." Scotty points.

William can't believe it, but there it is, a silver foil crown twisted on the poleman's head. The band changes songs, a deep rounded beat, the padded ends of the men's drumsticks ringing round and round the metal rims. The women sway, and the tiny man bends his dancing body, face to the sky, under the horizontal pole, emerging to the applause and delight of the audience.

William is confused. He watches the king lower the horizontal pole once, then twice more. Each time he succeeds in compressing his body under the pole, he lifts his sober, scrunched face toward the crowd, and William watches it transform into a radiant smile that makes the little man's eyes curve upward grinning. One by one he sheds his silver cape, his pants, his shirt. The long silver gloves go flying toward the women. Finally the king is dressed in just a pair of silver underpants. Before his final go-through, he takes a flaming torch from one of the women and lights first the vertical poles and then the crosswise one which he has lowered to a height that even William could not crawl under. The audience is still. The bleachers have ceased their creaking. Beside William, Natife comments in a faint, unintelligible voice. William can feel the weight of his mother's eyes on him. He turns to look at her, and they are caught by each other's eyes at the moment the king slides his bent form beneath the bar. The crowd hoots and whistles. William sights a large winged bird above them, heading away from Oak Hollow Park, higher and higher. He follows the steadfast meander of the bird's path. When he brings his eyes back down to earth, the little man on stage is holding up a cassette tape.

"Eight ninety-five," he says, pointing to a table set up beside the bleachers.

He is *not* a king, William thinks.

While Scotty climbs down the bleachers with Bernie watching her and Natife waiting to follow,

William races ahead. He pushes through the dispersing crowd and onto the stage. Although someone has taken away the cross stick, they've left the vertical poles standing. William sets himself between them, feeling the residual heat in lines down both sides of his body. For a moment he has a doubt. Maybe the man is a king. One would have to be very brave to stand between fire. He closes his eyes. The poles are fiery lances, and he has become a king who has survived an enemy attack. When William opens his eyes Natife is kneeling quietly in front of him. The drummers, packing up their equipment, are staring at them curiously.

"Come, William," Natife says. "Your mother is ready."

They are all subdued on the way back to Chalwright. Since it's Saturday and there's no real need for Natife and Bernie to return right away, Scotty decides to stop at the house to check on Goodwood. It's a spur-of-the-moment thing, and William can tell she is nervous. His father won't be there to greet them, showing off his record collection or the cozy nooks of the house he built with, as he says, "my own two hands." Sure enough Goodwood has managed to get to the screen door. They can see him lying miserably thwarted on the tiles of the foyer. Scotty opens the door carefully, and they all squeeze through the small opening.

"Oh, poor baby," Scotty says, leaning down to pick up Goodwood.

"Let me," Bernie says.

For a moment his mother and big Mr. Kennedy are both wrapped around Goodwood. William thinks they look like a family with Goodwood as the baby. He is strangely disappointed when they separate. Before Scotty directs the way to the rejected dog bed, she instructs William in whispers to offer Natife a cold drink, some cookies.

William takes Natife into the kitchen. There are five cupcakes left from his party, and he puts one on a plate, sticks a candle in it, and brings it to Natife. Because his father and Laurel were having a cake for him, his mother decided to go with cupcakes for the party.

"Two cakes are too much," she had grumbled. "I don't care what she says."

There had already been one argument about who would get William for the actual birthday. Two days before William's birthday, Greg had taken him to Laurel's house for a celebration. Laurel had bought the cake from Safeway, and, although it had Ninja Turtles and was frosted in blue, William didn't like it. He ate one bite and mashed the rest slowly with his fork while Benny and Keith ate theirs and fought over who would get to keep the turtle figures from the top of the cake.

"It's William's birthday," his father had said, "and his cake too, boys, remember. On your birthday you can keep the figures."

"Yeah, but we have to share," Benny said. "Shouldn't William share too, Mom?"

"Yeah," Keith chimed in.

"Well," Laurel had said, "there are four figures,

aren't there now?" Laurel was a psychologist, tall and blond, with a disconcerting habit of always smiling, even when William knew she must be angry.

"Laurel," Greg said, "it's William's birthday."

"I don't care," William said. "I don't want any. They can have them."

"William," his father said, "you don't have to give Benny and Keith your turtles you know. It is up to you."

William had kept his face down. He would not cry. "I hate Ninja Turtles," he said. "They're stupid. Can I go home now?"

His father had wanted him to open his presents first. Benny and Keith gave him Transformer Turtles. Laurel, with her teeth showing, gave him a book called *I Have Two Families Now* and a photograph of Benny and Keith with Laurel and Greg. His dad gave him a wooden sword he had made himself. William took the sword and went to the car where he sat until his father came out, jingling keys and motioning to the other vehicle in the driveway. Slowly William climbed out of his father's car and into Laurel's minivan. On the way home William rolled down his window and threw the sword out. His father stopped the car and backed up. He retrieved the beautifully crafted sword and tossed it into the back of the minivan beside Benny and Keith's muddy rubber boots.

Natife waves his hand over his cupcake, and the candle lights up. William smiles and walks to the table, sliding into a chair. He is about to ask Natife how he did that when his mother calls from upstairs.

"William," his mother calls down, "I'm going to give Bernie a tour of the house. Natife, come up if you want."

"A small trick," Natife says.

"My mom tells me all the time that life is full of tricks, and I should learn as many as I can so no one can pull them on me," William says.

Actually she has said this only once, shortly after she and Greg quit therapy with Laurel and not long before Greg packed his tools and clothes and the little blue braided rug that used to lie in the third-floor studio. But William likes the sound of extreme words: *forever, all the time, never again*.

Natife eats his cupcake icing first, just as William does. William appreciates the way Natife's hair stays motionless unlike his own which seems magnetized toward the icing.

"This," Natife says, "is a different kind of trick. It is *for* you. Not *on* you."

Then Natife asks, "Why does your mother keep carrying the dog upstairs?"

"He's dying. It's hot outside."

"Sometimes," Natife says frowning, "comfort is not the best thing."

William pulls one of his new knights out of his pocket. "Would you like to see my castle?"

"Soon. I will finish my cake first, all right?"

"Sure," William says. He prances his wide-legged

knight across the kitchen table. "Natife, are there knights in Nigeria?"

"Yes. Certainly there are some. Although they do not wear the armor, of course. It is too sultry and wet."

"How do you know they're knights then?"

"They do battle, of course." Natife picks a few crumbs from the bottom of the paper cupcake wrapper. "You know that, William."

"But how do they become knights?"

"Ah, do you become? Or have you always been? Most of the knights in my country disguise themselves as simple ordinary souls—like yourself. But when the moment comes . . . well, then, there they are."

"Where?" William wants to know, and Natife, eating carefully around the edges of the cupcake, continues.

"Two men quarrel. They say to one another: 'Now you've done it. I will come back with my entire clan. We will wipe you and your ancestors off the earth.' If there is a knight nearby, he comes quickly in the night and builds his castle between the two clans. He straddles their borders so that one does not know where his lands end and the other's begin. For awhile it is an uncomfortable place for the knight. Stray arrows drift into his courtyard, and he must be careful of even his own safety, if you can believe that. But the knight has strong juju. His rights are older and more entrenched. He is the beloved of his ancestors, and they ring his castle with their songs so that the warring men grow confused, and eventually they forget their battles and go home."

The sound of music begins to waft down from upstairs: Welsh folksongs his mother used to play while she painted. William hasn't heard them in months. Bernie Kennedy's sweet tenor harmonizes with the distant music.

"They just give up?" William asks glancing upward.

"The choice is not their own. By making war they've traded away their senses. They are transfixed. Then along come those—my new friend Bernie is one—known as *griots* to help ease the combatants into understanding. They tell stories of knights and battles. They sing songs."

"Like a troubadour," William interjects knowingly.

Natife nods and goes on. "The songs instruct: *Go home. Cease your foolish squabbling. Brave men know when to turn their backs on a setting sun. There is nothing for you here. Go home, go home.* And the men do. Later they honor the knight. They invite the griots into a sacred circle and toast them with palm wine."

William doesn't understand all of what Natife says, but he likes the idea of a knight as a king in disguise. He is impatient to show Natife his castle. He wants to know if there are castles like it in Natife's land, to ask him if he himself has ever met a knight.

Natife balls up his cupcake wrapper and puts it in his pocket. He follows William up the curved wooden stairs his father built when William was just a baby and used to sleep in his car seat amid the stacks of clear fir in the unfinished house. As they pass, Goodwood struggles to his feet and pulls himself off the dog bed and onto the oriental runner of the hallway. He shudders and raises himself on shaking legs until he covers another few inches of the hallway.

William's parents found Goodwood the spring they married. For years William has heard the story of the magical appearance of Goodwood. The little dog had wandered into the garage where Greg was getting his old Triumph fixed. The mechanics fed him the ends of their sandwiches, but no one wanted a dog. When Greg went to pick the car up, they'd stuck the dog inside with the repair order. A joke maybe, but Greg decided to bring him home for Scotty. In a way, Goodwood began their family long before William came along. William himself has a clear memory of toddling to his parents' room in the mornings and seeing the shaggy form lying protectively at the foot of their bed.

Twelve is perhaps not an ancient age for a Cairn terrier, but the cancer has aged Goodwood. His legs, once as sturdy as William's own, are spindly knobs with dull tufts of hair. When he tries to stand, his front legs shake and shudder, his rear legs refuse altogether. But he is persistent. He keeps his head down and breathes in thin wheezes that make William want to cover his ears and run outside.

William, his mother tells him, learned to walk with Goodwood. The little dog would stand patiently while William pulled at his fur, hoisting himself erect. Then slowly the two would move together around the living room like a pony in a ring at the carnival.

"C'mon, Natife," William tugs at his hand. "My room is right here." He can hear his mother laughing upstairs, a real laugh that makes William almost giddy.

But Natife has knelt down behind Goodwood and is watching the dog's labored progress toward what would seem to be a treacherous path, the winding wooden stairs. William heaves an exaggerated sigh, the put-upon sigh of a tired soul. He leaves his half-opened door and tramps down toward Goodwood. He gathers the dog uneasily in his small arms and trundles him back into the bed. William looks up then, satisfied that everything is okay now, that Natife will come and lie on his floor with him, moving knights and flinging lances about the castle walls. He is astonished to see Natife's face filled with grief.

"Look here, William," he says. "Here you see a noble battle."

William leans on the bedroom door, puzzled. Natife is crouched beside Goodwood, and William kneels beside him, looking back and forth from the dog to the young man. Although Natife has not said anything, William cannot help but feel he's been assigned a task, one that there is hope of his accomplishing, one that has been earmarked for him since birth. What the task is, though, William cannot guess. Goodwood grunts and struggles; Natife sits on his heels and opens his palms to the ceiling; William waits.

That night Scotty puts William to bed early and, humming, goes up to her studio to work for the first time in weeks. William falls asleep to the breathy wailing of her tape deck. He hears the shuffle of her feet and knows she is dancing as she paints. Twice in the night he wakes to Goodwood's groans and remembers Natife. His dreams are fretful. In an encampment, his soldiers sleep like the dead while he wanders through their ranks. As he passes beneath unlit torches, flames burst into life until the countryside is like an eerie fairyland, bewitched into restless peace. The night air is crisp but still. In the quiet he discerns the plaintive bellow of distant horns. They echo beseechingly, calling out to William. The third time he wakes up, the covers twisted beside him, it is because, finally, he understands.

The next morning William is up before it is completely light. He takes his quilt and a handful of knights and meets Goodwood by the door. The little dog gives out a muffled cry when William wraps him in the quilt and struggles with the door, but at last they are outside, and William has not yet dropped Goodwood. He carries him to the oak tree and releases him slowly. The dog sinks gratefully into a smooth space between two knobby roots. William curls up beside him. He encircles Goodwood with his knights facing outward, a protecting army. On second thought he widens the circle to include himself. He makes himself as small as he can, lies alongside the dying dog—a healthy addition to the heated misery of the animal—and pulls the quilt over them both. He hums to Goodwood, and, as the sky begins to clear away the night, William falls into the deep, dreamless sleep of a battle-weary warrior.

THE HIGHWAYMAN

In the early, silent dusk of a January afternoon, Coster drags a body from his mud-splashed car. The wind is blowing briskly, picking up whatever is not pinned down. The growing shadows are full of tumbling figures: leaves, forked twigs, and unidentifiable pieces of glowing white litter. Coster leans the man against the passenger door and then, in one astonishing movement, flips him over his narrow shoulder, displacing the figure's familiar-looking tan hat. My new friend, Lorraine, who has been keeping me company on this, my twenty-third birthday, joins me at the kitchen window.

"Pretty neat," Lorraine says. "You've married Hercules."

With her eyebrows raised and mouth pursed, Lorraine settles back into her chair to pour us each a little more rum from the nearly empty pint on the table.

"Here," she says, "I think we'll need this."

As we watch, the wind carries the stranger's hat to the sloping porch of the house, and just when Coster's fingers nearly touch its brim, the hat suddenly takes a sharp backward turn and sails past him toward the old barn on the other side of the lane.

"My father-in-law had a hat exactly like that," I say squinting as if the face of Coster's dignified father, long dead but immortalized in photographs around Coster's family home, might suddenly come into focus peering over his son's shoulder.

Coster zigzags awkwardly across the gravel road toward the barn, listing slightly under the weight of the body. Dressed garishly in a pair of madras pants and an odd lightweight jacket, the unknown figure appears to be both barefoot and unconscious.

"Another one of your husband's pals," Lorraine says.

Oh, please, I pray to myself, *not another one.*

Coster's acquaintances are a bruise on our new marriage, a continual sore spot that threatens what I remember the Reverend Doctor Newburgh, Coster's professor, calling the *sanctity of our union,* a phrase that I persist in translating as the *sanctuary of our union,* imagining a small, safe room where Coster and I are alone, away from the pounding insistence of his future flock which even at this moment appears to be gathering, ready to shove me aside.

Coster tries—usually. He rarely brings his new friends to the house, even though he continues to befriend strangers, odd losers who call late at night to talk about everything from their long-estranged families to the philosophies of Reinhold Niebuhr. He *should* be a minister, I try to tell myself on those nights when I wake up to hear Coster's soothing voice murmuring into the kitchen telephone. I hear the words in my head—calm, mature—as I shred a widening hole in the ratty blue blanket one of his fans knitted for us.

"They're all in love with you," I've complained to Coster. "I feel like your mother screening calls from your girlfriends."

Coster always shrugs, the easy humility of the beloved. "I talk with them," he tells me. "Most people don't."

But there's more to it, I know. When bums pass us on the street, they greet Coster by name and eye me suspiciously, and I can see how Coster's gray eyes brighten when he shoots the breeze with his riffraff friends. At those times he forgets that I am waiting for him, and gets caught up in animated discussions that show off his companions' broken-toothed smiles, their filthy, gesturing hands, which sometimes are missing whole fingers.

"Bottom feeders," Lorraine calls the lost souls who gravitate around Coster.

"They're all good guys," Coster will insist.

"Oh yeah, angels, I'm sure," I sigh. "They're using you," I finally tell him.

"Kit, honey," Coster says looking at me with all the earnestness he usually shows the bums. "Trust me.

There's no such thing as *using* someone. Someday they'll be there for me."

"And the dead shall rise up from their graves," I intone in my best future-minister's-wife's voice.

Now, his back bent low, my young husband slips in front of the next strong breeze to rescue the hat as it lands on the steps to the barn apartment where our neighbor, Buddy Dwyer, a musician, lives. The edges of our small yard and the corners of the barn have collapsed into shadow, and I can just make out the bald head of Coster's friend shining eerily in the pale light the musician keeps burning above his door.

"Five bucks says Coster drinks coffee with the Highwayman and doesn't even know it," Lorraine says, referring to the murderer who stalks our area. The newspapers have dubbed him "The Highwayman" because he frequents quiet country roads and strikes in darkness, usually the loneliest hours of early morning.

I am about to tell Lorraine not to be so stupid when Coster opens the door and shrugs his companion onto the living room couch and I see that the figure is not my father-in-law nor even one of Coster's angels, but a giant doll: a placid faced, floppy limbed mannequin with small pink breasts just barely visible under the safari jacket.

"Happy birthday, honey!" Coster says, breathing heavily.

"Wow!" Lorraine can't stop laughing. "You're

giving her a *body* for her birthday! What did I tell you, Kit? This guy has connections to the underworld."

"You always think so highly of me." Coster raises his head toward Lorraine with his shy grin. "Does he look like a criminal to you?"

"*He?* Oh, Cos-ter," Lorraine sings, poking one finger at the front of the safari jacket. "I think I have some bad news."

"Well, yes," Coster says, acknowledging the breasts with a shrug. "But dressed up like this who can tell?"

Lorraine fingers the madras pants. She's a small round woman with black curly hair and plain sallow features. A plain woman really, but so animated no one can stop looking at her when she's in the room. "He looks like a schizophrenic golf pro," she says. "You know, one of those guys who can't decide whether he's a piece of fruit or a big game hunter."

Coster lifts the hat from the body's head to his own. He doesn't look like anybody's savior now, just a tall, gangly guy with a sweet smile. "They were my dad's. Remember, Kit, we picked up those cartons from Mom's?"

I feel my mouth open, but no words come out. Lorraine hoots at the expression on my face and reaches over to pat my hand. "He is cute, though," she says eyeing the body. "Like a species as yet unnamed. Hey, Kit, what's your father-in-law's name?"

"Rollin," I tell her. "Rollin Eickenberry. But he's dead now."

"Perfect. We'll call this a resurrection." She dips her fingers in her glass and sprinkles rum over the body's slumped form. "I dub you Rollin, Knight Consort of Kit."

As she waves her hand from side to side, Lorraine brushes the curtain of the window beside the body, revealing the blue shadows of the encroaching evening.

"Oh my, Cinderella," she says, "it's pumpkin time again. Hey, wouldn't it be great if all the men turned into mice when you were done with them? Night falls and you take a broom and sweep them out the door."

Terrific, I think. Then we'd have yards full of rabid mice, and we'd still be afraid to go out at night.

Grimacing at the thought, I raise my head and meet Coster's eyes. In his gaze I read concern as well as the effort he's making on my behalf not to lecture Lorraine. And what does he see in *my* eyes? Does he imagine that, like him, I believe in the hope-heavy cause of resurrection, in retrievable goodness? In between his graduate classes at the theological school he works at the Center, supposedly doing simple office work. *Processing*, they call it. *Intake*. An appropriate term if I've ever heard one, since that is exactly what Coster is doing. He is bringing them all in. I sigh and Coster misreads that too, giving me a conspiratorial wink and turning his attention back to Lorraine, who is pulling on her jacket.

As I close the door behind Lorraine, I trip over the body's outstretched bare foot.

"Watch your step," says Coster catching me by the elbow just in time to save me from falling into the figure's lap.

Watch your step. The phrase has been ringing in my ears nonstop since November when the first body appeared and talk of the Highwayman began. Three bodies, all women, found dead in as many months. On my daily trek to work in the winter-darkened dawn, I scan the perimeter of the road in nervous anticipation. I buy newspapers and study the victims' photographs, looking vaguely for a link between the women and myself: a cocktail waitress; a high-school student driving an early morning newspaper route; a librarian who, during a fight with her husband, managed to grab the car keys and escape into the sweet emptiness of night. Is it any wonder that, although I'm technically free to browse the January sales or catch a movie at the Tri-Plex during my long, empty afternoons, I speed home instead, latching the doors and curling directly into the layers of blankets I drag around this perpetually chilly house?

My body—Rollin—reclines awkwardly on our only piece of living-room furniture all throughout the next day. He is there, too, when I trail off to bed that night during one of Coster's angel calls, but early Monday morning when I shuffle to the kitchen, wincing as I flick on light switches, the body is nowhere to be seen and I nearly forget about him—that is, until I head outside. Coster must have carried him out last night while I was asleep because there he is—Rollin the Body—waiting for me in the Ford Falcon that was a legacy from my Aunt Cici. With one arm draped along the red vinyl seatback and his head tilted slightly to one side, Rollin looks as if he's engaged in an important conversation. I can almost see my aunt leaning into the body's half-embrace, before letting loose one of her deep-throated laughs. I feel strange slipping into the driver's seat beside him, as if I might be letting him down by not being someone more lively, someone like Cici. I lock the doors and let the Falcon warm up. While I'm waiting I readjust the body so that his hands are folded demurely in his lap. That *he* is really a *she* doesn't matter to me. Lorraine's christening has transformed the body into maleness, and swathed in his new wardrobe, sitting tall on two telephone books, Rollin looks the part almost entirely.

Aside from the porch light which I leave burning, all the surrounding buildings are dark. On the way down the long gravel driveway, I'm pierced by a sharp flutter of anxiety when I spot a lone figure shambling toward me, but it's just Buddy Dwyer, the musician who lives above the barn. I wave at him. He hoists his guitar case into the air slightly and nods wearily. Our musician neighbor lost his license on a DUI shortly after we moved here last fall after our wedding, and he must count on strangers, including Coster once or twice, for rides. Sometimes it seems he has to walk all the way home from his gigs.

The forty-minute drive to work is uneventful and

beautiful. Stars choke the sky and the half-moon follows me from curve to curve, filling my car with blue-tinged light and making Rollin's pale skin shine like a fragile alien.

"You're not from around here, are you, Mister?" I find myself saying to the body, lifting the brim of the sailing hat to steal a gaze at the blank face. I am surprised to find it sweet and strangely calming.

My birthday present. *So what did your husband give you for your birthday, Kit?*

Although I have told myself over and over again that I don't care for birthdays, I can't help feeling let down as I slide back into the work week, my special day behind me.

"You know," I inform Rollin, "if Aunt Cici was still alive everything would have been completely different."

Take, for example, my sixteenth birthday. I was new to town and friendless, and Cici invited every shop clerk within a week's worth of errands, guaranteeing a newfound batch of acquaintances for me. My aunt's enthusiasm took me offguard, but our guests easily followed Cici as she led us all through a series of parlor games.

Aloud I say to Rollin, "What a party that was!"

"I haven't played Spin the Bottle in forty years," declared Martha, the crabbiest of the cashiers at the local Foodtown, even as she expertly tipped the bottle toward a genial Foodtown butcher, the one who put aside meaty bones for Cici's standard poodle, Lamont. Nethalie and Thor from the lumberyard played Truth or Dare against Post Office Ida and Werner from the Sweet Pickle Deli. All of us took part in Charades, an activity at which my actress aunt excelled. At cake-cutting time Cici demanded that our guests produce their gifts. She had requested that each write a birthday wish for me and bring it to the party. For my part, she handed me a short stack of pink notes on which I was instructed to list my fears. Afterward I was supposed to rip up the pink papers into one of her big glass mixing bowls, which she placed expectantly on my lap. Coincidentally many of my fears seemed directly to counter the wishes thrust my way.

May men swarm all over you, one note read just after I'd scrawled the word *Men* on one of the pale pink notes Cici had handed me.

Leaving here, I wrote on another only to open the next wish: *May you travel all over the world and see great sights.*

Only when the bowl was full of confetti ready to fling into the air, I tell Rollin, would Cici let us eat the cake. While the checkers and clerks forked in the poppy-seed cake Cici had frosted heavily with lemon icing and decorative, but inedible, silver balls, my aunt looked hard at me and scribbled her own wish—one simple word: *Trust*—on a nearby scrap.

Rollin's face, calmly expectant, flashes by me briefly as the car moves under a streetlight. I change the subject. I tell him about Coster, how he's bent on saving the world, one soul at a time. Rollin's head tilts sympathetically. *What else?* he seems to ask.

I describe my job, apologizing as I do for the early hours.

The body has a contented smile that thrills me. Rollin is a find. He is the perfect guest, fascinated by me, his hostess. *How pleasant for you,* his upturned face declares. *How absolutely wonderful. Tell me, tell me more.* And I do.

From five-thirty until ten each weekday morning, I sit in the almost empty Morristown unemployment office, a single-level brick building with smoky, tinted windows on an asphalt lot surrounded by a ten-foot-high chain link fence. Together with Lorraine, I take sick calls from public school teachers throughout Morris County. We listen to their strained excuses, jot down their instructions, and then, from the list of approved substitute teachers, fill the vacancies. Most of our work consists of waking people up, cajoling them into taking on a class for the day. Hardly ever do I have what could be termed a conversation with the teachers—although Lorraine usually manages a few one-sided cracks. By nine o'clock the regular full-time staff of job counselors and unemployment clerks has arrived and our job is nearly done. All that remains is an hour of lazy paperwork eked out at the snail's pace the State of New Jersey demands.

Lorraine is new. This is only her second month on the job and she has an easy attitude about the position. She doesn't, for instance, arrive at the empty office at five-thirty in the morning dressed for success, although we are officially climbing the ladder. The last

Teacher's Registry counselors have gone on, we've been told, to become permanent staff.

"Shoot me," Lorraine shuddered after hearing that news, "if I ever aspire to such a promotion."

As if to forestall that possibility, each morning she arrives in the same sweats and T-shirt she sleeps in, and holds off changing into a black skirt and one of her many turtlenecks until after our seven o'clock run for coffee and buttered Kaiser rolls, an innovation to the routine that Lorraine initiated and insists upon. Lorraine also considers it her duty to gossip about the office and the voices on the telephone.

"I like to know who I'm dealing with," she explains. "So what's the story with the creep in the hairpiece?" She nods toward the empty desk to her right, the one belonging to Alphonse Riddley, one of the full-time job counselors. Each day Riddley spends his first working hour staring morosely at Lorraine as she shuffles through the morning's batch control reports.

"He breeds dachshunds," I say, repeating the only information I've gleaned about the man and setting off an infectious spiral of laughter in Lorraine. Even Janitor William, a dignified, lonely figure to whom I have barely spoken before, comes out of his supply room to lean on Riddley's desk and laugh with us.

Between phone calls Lorraine pulls information out of me. Days before she met him, she knew the story of Coster's privileged upbringing, his magnetic attraction toward the homeless, and, before our first week together was out, I also told her how I had closed down in high school. For weeks at a time I'd come home from school and slink back into bed. There I constantly reworked my algebra homework, the same problems over and over again, until I'd worn the notebook paper through with my erasing. It was the only homework I attempted, believing that at least in math I could find one right answer. But I could no more factor a polynomial than I could shake off the inexplicable weight that clutched me just below my throat.

"I see," Lorraine said. "And then?"

Sitting quietly at her desk for once, she gave me all her attention. I kept going, telling her how after nearly an entire semester of this, my befuddled parents, lacking the resources and knowledge to send me to a real therapist, did the next best thing and sent me to live with Aunt Cici who had played a psychiatrist in a Bucks County Playhouse production that my parents had seen years ago. At that Lorraine's serious demeanor finally cracked. "Not bad," she said, "not bad at all."

That first afternoon with Rollin I avoid the crush of Morristown after work, choosing to meander home down a series of back roads. The peculiarly mild winter continues with its relentless drizzle. The old Falcon's wipers rattle and whine as they smear the rain back and forth across the windshield, but for once the sound doesn't unnerve me. I flick the radio switch and sing along with the corny country-western station that comes in better than any other. Secretly I love this music, full of wailing passion and inevitable loss. I stop for gas in Bernardsville and dive back into the wooded lanes, yodeling about love gone wrong and a home that's always waiting. As I swing up the driveway past the old barn, I wonder if this is the sort of music our neighbor, Buddy Dwyer, plays.

The phone is ringing when I carry Rollin inside our rented carriage house, and it takes me a few moments to make the shift from Garth Brooks still playing in my head to the churlish voice whining in my ear. Of course he wants Coster, and my hesitation somehow convinces him that I'm lying when I tell him Coster isn't home.

"Lady," the man says as if *I'm* bothering *him*, "I'm only gonna take a minute."

"Listen, Mister," I am surprised to hear the fury under my words, "Coster can't talk to you because he's not here, and I'm not certain when he will be."

"Oh, sure," the man says. He pauses before continuing, "What kind of fucking newlywed are you anyway? He's never there, huh? You're always alone, huh?" He softly curses me, and I slam the receiver down. Almost immediately it rings again, and my heart pounds so loudly the sound fills my ears, pushing out any memory of Garth Brooks. I gather Rollin in my arms and flee to the Falcon as the phone shrills behind us.

Before a few days go by, I have a morning routine with Rollin. I wrestle him from his place on the living room couch and settle him like an old friend beside me in the front seat of the Falcon. (The cold air deflates him,

I've discovered, so staying overnight in the car is out of the question.) My chats with Rollin on the way to work refresh me and keep me almost oblivious to the mounting danger of the Highwayman. According to the papers he tends to strike near the full moon, a little more than a week away. The phone calls continue, but the cursing man is not among them. Nonetheless I find the Falcon far more comfortable than home.

Without telling Coster, I also begin to take long drives in the evening with Rollin while Coster is at his seminars on ethics and family counseling. When I was a child I envied ghosts, how they could slip into even the most dangerous situations without a care. For no good reason I feel the same abandon with Rollin at my side. Sometimes I meet Lorraine for dinner at Panchechi's Pizza Palace, conveniently located downstairs from Lorraine's apartment in a decaying brick building in Bernardsville. Once we visit a huge bowling alley near a town I've never heard of, a town that Lorraine assures me is a lot of fun as she offers directions toward Rollin's steadfast head. A cocktail bar revolves in the center of the bowling alley. "So that you can't miss a thing on league night," Lorraine says while the scrawny bartender nods seriously, stroking Lorraine's hand until she slaps him, not hard but firmly, on the knuckles.

Most evenings, though, it's just the two of us, Rollin and I, winging our way down the expectant byways, the twisting back roads of Far Hills, Bedminster, and Bernardsville.

"You don't mind him much, do you Kit?" Coster

inquires two weeks after the body's arrival. It's breakfast time, really my usual lunch time, and Rollin slumps beside the front door, off duty for the weekend.

"Ummhmm," I mumble keeping my eyes on the pink grapefruit wobbling on my plate, all those little segments. "He's okay."

If I were truthful I would tell Coster that I've never had a friend like Rollin. One morning I cry all the way to work and he doesn't move. I don't need to explain that my tears have no immediate source but are simply a passing emotion washing over me as easily as a storm momentarily consumes the landscape. His kindly face tilts toward me as if to say, *So this is what you need to do.* And Rollin is as solitary as I. He waits for me, depending on me, Kit, for movement and conversation.

Not only that, but I grow convinced that miracles occur when he's around. Not huge lame-walking, blind-seeing miracles, but quieter loaves-and-fishes miracles. My car, for instance, hums like a top these days and gets, if my math is correct, seventy-two miles to the gallon. The flu rages through Morris County knocking whole school districts flat. Even Lorraine calls in sick one morning, but I remain untouched.

"I think I'm immune," I tell her among the stampede of teacher calls.

Sick as she is, Lorraine manages to cackle at me. "You're in love. And who wouldn't be, cruising with Harpo Marx all day?"

In gratitude I shop for Rollin on my free afternoons. I visit the hospital thrift store, the local tailor's shop, Bamberger's men's department. It's like the old days with Aunt Cici, cruising for costumes for her plays. I purchase worn but comfortable-looking turtlenecks, corduroys, a tweed jacket. I splurge on a plush deep green scarf the texture of cashmere; a comical but almost beautiful Russian hat with long fur earflaps; a pair of rubber overshoes. One day Rollin is a college professor; the next, an artist or a stockbroker. I even splash a little eau de cologne on the edge of his collar on the morning he is a salesman.

One Friday morning Coster wakes early, nauseous and fevered. He lurches into the bathroom and returns a few moments later, making it as far as the couch before he collapses, one hand over his forehead. An odd sight: my pale and disheveled husband lying next to my dapper companion. My coat already on, I creep toward them, unsure for a moment who I'm reaching for. I light on Rollin. Silently I will carry him away so that I can throw a cover over Coster who looks so still that I'm sure he'll sleep all morning.

"What is that?" Coster asks suddenly as I lift Rollin. "A trenchcoat?"

"A mackintosh. A Burberry knock-off. With that hat he looks a little like David Niven, don't you think?"

Coster's eyes flutter and close. I have a fleeting urge to undress and lie beside him and let his fever overtake me.

Instead I say, "Will you be okay?"

"I love you, Kit," my husband murmurs. "Do you know that?"

I nod slowly even though I know he can't see me.

"Wait," he says. "I just need a little rest. Then we'll talk."

He is nearly asleep, each word a new separate breath. His body—too thin these days; he never has time to eat—is a poor match for this illness. I can see him struggling to come awake again. There are things he wants to say, and I'd like to trust that I hear them beneath the hum of his fatigue. Oh but how hard I have to listen, and in the end I might have just imagined the words I want to hear. I kiss him and his eyes open briefly. He wants so much to be here to save me, to save everyone.

"Kit," he murmurs once more, then he's lost to me again. Rollin, heavy in my arms, shifts to one side, and I nearly lose my balance before I'm out the door and safely on my way to the Falcon.

In just a few hours schools are in session, and I'm back home, ready to nurse Coster through the afternoon. Every few hours, I bring him a spoonful of cold medicine that lures him away from me into sleep, even as he struggles to sip from the water glass I hold for him.

Afternoon inches into evening. The phone and its frantic bleating, the same hesitant, slurred voices: Coster's angels. Tired myself, I treat them delicately, and they are uncharacteristically acquiescent.

"Quiet," I say, "the man needs quiet."

"Yes, ma'am," they whisper to me as if making up for the telephone's ring.

As Coster sleeps I move through our silent house, shifting Rollin from room to room with me. At nine o'clock I call Lorraine. I put on my coat and whisper to my sleeping Coster that I'll be back soon, that he'll sleep and get well, that I love him too—*really*—but there's a hopelessness in my voice that even I can hear.

"What I don't get," Lorraine says shaking red pepper flakes onto a slice of Panchechi's pizza, "is how he gets into their cars."

The restaurant is oddly deserted for a Friday night, but we have been tucked into a back booth and the service is slow. We wait nearly forty minutes for our pizza.

"Subterfuge," I offer. "He hears the car and wanders into the center of the road, pretending to be hit. Then when she stops to help—"

"Nah. How could he know the car would be driven by a woman alone? Besides, would you stop? I'd run over anyone that even pretended to jump in front of my car. No," Lorraine shakes her head as she bites into the pizza, "he must follow them."

"Or else he's already in the car."

"But what about the librarian? How would he know she'd have a fight with her husband and fly out the door at three in the morning?"

When we run out of scenarios, Lorraine and I switch to profiling the killer. We pencil out a suspect list and head it with Alphonse Riddley who arrives each morning looking exhausted and thin-lipped, claiming that the dachshunds keep him awake. We take turns adding to our list. Lorraine names one of our substitutes—Frank Maldonado—a man with a lisping voice who we've been asked not to call for elementary school duty because he frightens younger children. I put the bartender from the bowling alley on the list. Lorraine nominates our waiter, a high-school kid with a shaved, pointed head and fingers that look like they've all been cut to the same length. Before we're done with our first slices of pizza, we have six men, all perfectly plausible suspects, and I've lost my appetite.

"Bites, doesn't it?" Lorraine says. "Even my parish priest seems like a possibility."

"Oh, don't start. Priests scare the hell out of me. Such soft hands."

Lorraine gives me one of her raised eyebrow looks and passes the wine bottle. "Interesting," she says. "Here, drink. Forget it. We'll go nuts if we start thinking every guy's the Highwayman. Hey, it could be a woman. Remember the cops found a suspicious hair elastic in that one car."

"Please," I groan. "You'll be on my list soon."

After dinner Lorraine stands on the sidewalk, observing as I replace Rollin in the passenger seat of the Falcon, untie and reknot a paisley tie around the body's neck, and brush lint off his corduroy jacket.

"Let me guess," Lorraine says. "He's an unemployed actor going for his first legitimate job interview since he decided he was a no-talent hack. He's off to the personnel department of AT&T where he'll laboriously fill out an application and take a typing test that he'll fail miserably. Yes?"

"You know what I'd like to do, Lorraine?" I say. "I'd like to drive out to the diner for pie and coffee. Aunt Cici and I used to buy the early edition of the weekend papers and work our way around the revolving pie rack: blackberry, cherry, key lime, lemon meringue, Boston cream."

When Lorraine doesn't answer me immediately, I turn to Rollin. "What do you think, Miracle Man? Are you up for it?"

After a pause Lorraine says quietly, "I know nothing of course, Kit, but do you think this might be getting out of hand? What's Coster think of Rollin these days? I see your husband sitting home with his head in his hands moaning, 'I've created a monster!' while you and the unemployed actor here are buying plane tickets to Cabo."

"A sixth-grade teacher," I correct, fitting a baseball cap on Rollin's head. "All the girls have crushes on him." I put on his seat belt and close the door gently. "Besides," I add, "he has the flu."

"Rollin?"

"Lorraine," I try to keep my voice as even as possible, "I'm talking about Coster."

"Whew." Lorraine slaps her hand on the side of the Falcon. "You had me worried there for a moment, honey." She smiles briefly, a wry self-mocking smile, before growing serious.

"Really, Kit, go home."

"Yeah, yeah," I say. "Of course."

The late-night waitresses are all older women. The one who brings me coffee places her hand briefly on my shoulder.

"Did you say blackberry or cherry on that pie, hon?"

The touch of her hand is so reassuring that I relax and begin to peruse the thin Saturday edition of the paper I grabbed off the stack by the register on my way to the booth. For a moment, as I separate the paper into sections, I'm joined by Cici, unwrapping one of her lengthy scarves, lighting a cigarette as she begins our communal read. *Kit, honey,* I think I hear her laugh, *listen to this.* My pie arrives and its sweetness mingled with the jolt of the coffee sets off a new jangle within me. Weekend section, comics, sports—I am building toward the real news when a man slides into the booth opposite me.

"Hey," Buddy Dwyer says, "I thought that was you."

I jump, I can't help it. My hand jerks and what is left of my coffee overturns. The waitress rushes over with a damp folded towel. The busboy, an older man who looks vaguely familiar, shambles over with a new paper placemat and napkin.

"It's okay," the waitress says. "It's slowed down so much we needed the excitement. Right, Harv?"

The busboy, a gnome in his fifties, grimaces at the

waitress, then eyes me as if he knows me too. To avoid his rheumy, searching gaze, I offer him a quick nod and drop my eyes to a raw-looking scratch on his right hand. Buddy Dwyer balls up a handful of coffee-soaked napkins, and the busboy takes them away with one last hard look, this time aimed at my neighbor.

"It is quiet, isn't it?" Buddy Dwyer says as he resettles his guitar case.

Although bustling when I entered shortly after midnight, the diner is nearly empty now. A pair of truckers roosts on stools, flirting with the other two waitresses. A few booths down an older couple steadily plows through two deluxe roast beef dinners. And way at the back of the diner in the last booth three teenagers flip through the tabletop jukebox, searching for ridiculous song titles and calling them out to one another. The diner's fluorescent lights make everyone appear slightly greenish, each pore and blemish revealed. I notice the busboy has moved to the foyer by the restrooms. I can't stop watching the way he clutches the pay phone. I know his look, have seen it plenty in the past year. He whispers fervently into the phone. One hand flies into the air. Finally he nods emphatically and puts the phone back on its hook. As he does he pivots and looks directly at me, directly *into* me, as if he knows absolutely everything about me and does not like one thing. Automatically I add him to Lorraine's list.

Buddy Dwyer calls me back. "Didn't mean to startle you," he says.

I've never been so close to the musician before. Coster once shared a beer with him, leaning on the truck we'd borrowed to move to our rental house, but I, eager to set up house, had been busily unpacking cartons inside. I am amazed in fact that, given our limited acquaintance, Buddy Dwyer could recognize me. I tell him so. Now Buddy is the one taken off guard.

"Have you been playing somewhere?" I ask.

"Well, it is Friday night," Buddy says. "And you? What's . . . Oscar? . . . doing letting you out by yourself?"

His eyes, I decide, are his best feature—feverishly bright, almost terrifyingly direct, but still very appealing. I am surprised. With his long fair hair and delicate face, he's like a character out of one of Cici's plays, a younger brother betrayed by his own family. For the first time, I wonder about Buddy Dwyer's private life, the apartment over the barn. I know from Coster that the musician has a drinking problem, but I can't imagine him drunk—not with those eyes.

"Poor Coster," I say. "He's so medicated he'll probably sleep until Tuesday."

Buddy reaches over and brushes a sticky crumb from my cheek. The motion of his finger makes my skin burn, and I stop talking. Several seconds pass before our conversation resumes—Buddy admiring my earrings, me asking questions about his gig. We chat almost like old friends, our conversation only slightly stilted by the awkward fact that we don't really know each other.

The waitress leans over me with another full pot of coffee. "Ready for another hit?"

I cover my cup with my hand. "I think I'd better call it quits. Look at my hands." I hold my fingers out so that they tremble slightly.

"Suit yourself," the waitress says, slipping me her check before turning to Buddy. "How about you? Ready for your usual?"

"Ah, keep me company," Buddy begs me, his voice slightly mocking. "I thought you said he'd sleep until Tuesday."

"He'll worry in his sleep," I say. "You know Coster."

Abruptly Buddy sits back against the brown vinyl booth. "Okay then," he says as if dismissing me. "Maybe I'll see you on the road later."

Suddenly it dawns on me that Buddy doesn't have a car. I imagine his solitary figure stalking through the fog for miles. He reads my uneasy face.

"Oh, it's okay," he says with a tight smile as if I've offered him the ride. "There's always somebody going my way."

Two state troopers have entered the diner behind me while I've been sitting with Buddy. Hips heavy with guns and radios, they balance on stools near the register where I wait to pay my check. The policemen's eyes pass over me while Harv, the busboy, casts furtive glances in my direction. I fumble my change back in my wallet. I offer a terse wave to Buddy, who gives me a distracted frown in return. Then I turn toward the door and there is Coster. The scream that rises in my throat fills the diner, causing the state troopers to swivel on their stools and clutch their guns.

If the lighting in the diner makes everyone else look merely sick, Coster is the walking dead. His coat is unzipped and I can see that he managed only a rag of a T–shirt over his jeans. His neck is flushed a deep red below his pale face.

He says nothing when I go to him, just hugs me so tightly I think we both will break. Beneath his thin jacket he's hot and damp, and when he lets me go he nearly collapses. It's all I can manage to lean him against a booth before Harv the busboy arrives to support him. Together we help Coster toward the door.

A trooper rises to hold the door for us. "You all right, miss?" he asks, eyeing me doubtfully as I nod.

"Just a sick man," Harv says quickly. "She's got it under control."

"Okay, Harv," the trooper says.

The lot had been full earlier and I'd parked away from the highway, back toward the trees by the diner's kitchen door. Coster's Volvo is pulled beside the Falcon where a spotlight above the dumpster illuminates the ridiculous figure of Rollin, sitting tall. Harv doesn't bat an eye at the body. He tosses Rollin into the backseat where he lounges like an amiable drunk, then together we ease Coster into the car. As I wait for the old Falcon to warm up, I watch the busboy. Instead of returning inside, Harv leans against the back wall of the diner and lights a cigarette with an odd backhand motion that makes me recognize him immediately as one of Coster's angels. He drank coffee with us one day in the park and lit cigarette after cigarette with that same crooked gesture. I roll down my window to thank him for phoning Coster, but Harv just shakes his head and, exhaling smoke, waves me away.

"Goodnight now, Mrs. Coster," he says. "You go home now."

A CLOSED SEA

THEY CARRIED HER FROM THE INLAND SEA TO PORT HOPE on their shoulders, in their arms, or between them like a fellow pilgrim. Her light brown hair tangled in the buttons of their jackets, and they whispered apologies as they shifted her from man to man. She was tiny, at first some said weightless, but any journey adds substance. Each evening they were exhausted as dark crowded among them. Still they did not stop, having learned that halting brought no rest. Instead they slept on their feet, waiting for moonrise and second winds.

The main bearer was a man named Samuel, like the others from a fishing village on the eastern edge of the country. A huge man who dwarfed his compatriots, Samuel cried as he walked, tears soaking his shirt collar and the girl's uncovered brow. She could have been one of his daughters, even Flavia, so wild and alive. Of course the girl herself never made a sound. She was beyond that, her eyes barely flickering when the men began to sing, spurred on by Peter, the elderly tenor. If such songs were unseemly, if they broke the unwritten rules of manly decorum, no one thought to complain.

Samuel was used to broken nights and sleep fractured by worry. Flavia often awakened him as she crept through a downstairs window, her hair messy with bracken, her skirt twisted and mud-stained. What do you do with a daughter like that? Rave like a lunatic, switch in hand? Dozing in his chair by the open window Samuel would feel the night breeze shiver on his arms and imagine Flavia swimming the river to the sea, turning back only when the surf began to roar in her ears. Always she gave a little jump as she cleared the window ledge, but rather than tiptoe past holding her breath as his younger girl, Josie, might have done, Flavia would come directly to him and remove his cold pipe from where it had fallen on the rise of his chest. Then she would kiss him lightly on the cheek.

"Oh, Papa," she'd say, sighing with her mother's voice.

If Flavia was the family adventurer, her sister Josie was the opposite: a hearth girl who flinched at every excursion that took her from home. Early each morning, when he saw her striking off toward the lonely pasture with their Holstein, Rita, Samuel noted Josie's rushed step, her tight hand on the cow rope, and he swore at himself for allowing this deep pocket of unease to nestle in his sensitive girl.

As he and his companions tramped through the

night, Samuel's thoughts raced ahead to his daughters. Often Samuel wished he could set his girls down and rearrange their qualities: shade Flavia's wicked abandon with Josie's caution; temper Josie's dreaminess with the cunning of adventure. "I haven't a wish in the world," he sometimes declared to his fellow fishermen. But that wasn't true. It was obvious how he mooned after his girls, scheming to hold them close. It was that, his one great desire, which had led him to this journey in the first place.

At first the villagers had not known what to make of the whispers or the stranger who set up his display reverently in the village square and verified the rumor that had preceded him. Yes, a closed sea, he told them, hidden inland and rich with every imaginable fish. The stranger himself was a familiar sort, a humble fisherman like themselves, and he rushed to tell them that the artifacts lying at his feet on a swath of heavy foreign cloth were not his own discoveries. They had been given to him by another man who had in turn been selected by yet another to tell the tale in this part of the country.

Unbelievably the villagers seemed to recognize these objects.

"I *know* that," old Claude told his wife, pointing to a curlicued shell that looked as if it were made of swirled pink glass.

"Sea dust," murmured another, giving name to a cupful of iridescent sand.

And the waxy, domed water flowers that opened and closed as if breathing, sending the suggestion of perfume into the crowd?

"Yes, yes," voices came together in agreement. These too were familiar. Heads were scratched, beards pulled. Then the villagers fell silent because what they knew was neither great enough for remembrance nor faded enough to ignore. But a week later a second messenger arrived, clutching his own natted blanket and *its* otherworldly contents, and old tales of a closed sea began reappearing with dramatic speed. Ancient women tilted their heads coquetishly and crooned long-forgotten ballads, while the knees of the fishermen grew weak with desire for the legendary sea where one could cast away sorrows and retrieve the grandest of dreams.

Maybe if it had not been the storm-ridden winter months when only madmen braved the willful winds; perhaps if the strangers had arrived in midsummer when the fish runs were heavy and the men were wistful for comfort; then in all likelihood their yearning would not have been so great. As it was, they were weary of sitting around. Their muscles ached from lack of use, and they tired easily of the voices of their families. For awhile they continued to weave new ropes and scrape hulls thick with barnacles, but after more strangers arrived with *their* bundles, lights began to appear in windows at all hours of the night, and in the boatyards the sounds of chisels and saws hummed noisily beneath the wind. Lanterns darted back and forth as if a grand navy were being equipped. Of course they could not go by water. Everyone knew that. Yet the need to be prepared was so overwhelming that no man could content himself with winter lap tasks. Instead each plunged headlong into readiness, already imagining himself afloat on water the shifting colors of a peacock's eyefeathers.

In the beginning Samuel resisted the lure. When his wife's illness had crept into his house, he had been blind, caught up in the daily tumult of the fishing season. She managed to hide the tremors and faints, to cajole the girls into fooling him with their nascent attempts at housewifery until it was too late. All his bargains with God had gone unanswered, and Samuel for one no longer believed he had any illusions about a paradise on earth.

And yet . . . one night shortly after talk of the inland sea re-emerged, Samuel dreamed he set Flavia and Josie into a little boat. In the dream his girls were children again, their bright yellow hair braided into the elaborate loops his wife favored for holidays. They waved giddily to him as he stood on the beach, before hoisting their tiny sail and bobbing away. He paced the shore keeping the sail in sight, fearful of the instant when it would slip over the horizon. But that moment never arrived. The sea was an egg in Samuel's dream, and its smooth sides led his girls back to him again and again.

The villagers were neither poor nor rich. Need did not chase them forth. Nor were any of them born risk-takers. So why then, why did all of them, even old Claude, show up at the plaza when the fourth visitor (a woman peddler, her head swathed with blue and purple scarves) appeared, bearing nothing but a rude map? And why were tempers nearly lost as men and women vied for a place in the traveling party? Straws were produced to guarantee fairness, but when the all-male party was chosen a riot nearly broke out with children whining and even Flavia railing at her own dear papa. Still, good manners were well ingrained. The tumult dissipated quickly. Haste took its place. They must be off—at once! At once!

Of the journey itself nobody could recall much besides the blurred passing of days, a nose-to-the-ground tracking of the map. They fit their obedient feet into the wide ruts of the footpaths and ignored the wind that followed them through every turn. They met no one, gabbled like children among themselves, ate salted fish from a shared pouch. At night they lay their cheeks against the rough cloth of their makeshift packs and slept in a ring around a tidy fire.

Five men, all dreaming. Old Claude and Alphonse—for these two only money would suffice, vast pots of it, gilded and uncountable. Old Claude had his young wife to think of, all her clanging desires, while Alphonse, young himself and often dismissed, itched for the respect that fortune could bring. Of the others, Peter, the palsied singer, wanted his voice back; Clive, town know-it-all, would have his mind's storehouse inexhaustible, facts ready on the tongue;

Samuel could think only of his daughters—Josie with her crippling fear and Flavia whose lust for the river and the night must spell disaster. His wife had liked to say that fears were just wishes in reverse, but for Samuel both were muddled inextricably.

The map's route bade them leave the road repeatedly until they could no longer tell whether the road they emerged upon was regained or altogether new. They pierced a dense grove of skinny alders, circled a marsh before arriving finally at sand dunes the length and breadth of a miniature mountain range. For every foot they gained, it seemed they lost two. Sand poured into their boots. Samuel held old Claude on one side, poor Peter on the other, and charged on relentlessly. Finally, heads pounding from the effort, eyes weakened by the constant assault of the snowlike landscape, they achieved the summit.

Inexplicably, for the first several moments as they stood poised on the final hill, not one man noticed the sea. Instead their attention was riveted by a figure on the shore, who waved his arms wildly in their direction, shouting words they could barely hear. Clive, somber Clive, christened "Professor," let loose a sharp cry. He claimed to be the doubter and had been anxious to come if only to prove them wrong. At the beginning of their journey he had listed for them the names of other supposedly closed seas: Pontus Euxinus, the Khorezm, Marmara with its marble quarries—all of them had turned out to be fakes. There was the far-off Caspian of course, but that too was nothing more than a pretender, sinking daily as rivers stole away its waters and men raked its riches of caviar and herring. This other sea, the closed sea they sought, must be a fairy tale as well. That was what he had said, but now Clive was the first to glance past the man, and it was Clive jumping up and down, ripping off his old black hat and sending it drifting into the air, Clive shouting *Hurrah! Hurrah!* and racing down the crumbling slope as if he would embrace the waving man, nearly ripping his trousers in his haste. And there, as far as the eye could follow, was a pale sea with a golden shimmer, its great waves cresting grandly toward their ordinary feet. A sweet scent like overripe pears swept over them. They were, they each realized, ravenous to the point of delirium.

Before long the party faced a narrow-featured man whose curling mustaches seemed to emphasize the closed-fist gestures he had used to beckon them closer to the shore. Alphonse began to unbutton his shirt, eyeing the water with undisguised longing, but the little man with the mustaches shook his head, his lips twisting into what Alphonse imagined was a taunt.

"No one knows what will happen," the man said, his voice slightly trembling.

He himself had stumbled on the closed sea, had not done more than drift along in a boat he found on the shore. No wind, he swore, the boat moved of its own accord. He had dared to dip one hand in the water and found it to be neither salty nor fresh, but spiced. Like cinnamon or ginger. One sip and he was gone.

When he regained consciousness his borrowed boat was beached and filled with chubby fresh-caught fish.

This is what he told the men, but Samuel noticed his cheek twitching and did not trust him.

White fish, the man informed them, grinning slyly. He had some left yet. White fish like nothing ever tasted. He opened his fists to the men and offered them his precious catch. Oh, they were hungry! They'd never desired food so much. Each man took except Samuel who looked past the man to the beached boat, which seemed to quiver slightly despite the still air. A faint memory of his dream stirred within him, and Samuel raced toward the boat, half-expecting to find his children inside.

The other men had barely swallowed the fish the man gave them when Samuel reached the boat. He noticed the girl's hair first, that light brown, flowing over the boat's wooden side, and his heart nearly collapsed with relief. Then he realized the girl's condition. The stranger tried to hold him back, but no magic fish flesh could match Samuel's strength. Under a rough blanket her legs were embedded with jewels and blood. What horror, he thought, the man has carved her legs for their riches. But no, not jewels—the girl's bare legs were covered in scales. And yet she was alive! Her chest, that of a young girl, shuddered for breath. He did not hesitate but covered the girl quickly—that same heavy cloth—and went after the man.

Perhaps only a father could understand. His companions were in shock, seeing the blood on Samuel's hands. Alphonse called out weakly in protest, but Samuel was unstoppable, and the man seemed to acquiesce as if acknowledging the depth of his crime. Samuel's fellow travelers couldn't move at first. Finally they too peered in the boat and saw the girl, her apricot cheek as lifeless as a doll. Her legs. Without saying a word they came together and buried the stranger beyond the sea dust under a common sand dune.

That quickly their dreams were dashed.

The sea swept away, away, farther than their eyes could follow, not the sapphire of the old tales, but a muddy gold that seemed almost to vanish into the sandy shore. It hurt the fishermen to look. Despite their fatigue, the horrible lingering sweetness in their mouths, all were anxious to crawl back up the sand dune toward home. But the girl. Their backs to the boat, they argued over what to do.

How could they leave her? They who had tasted her flesh? But how, too, could they take her home with them?

"Never mind," Samuel said. "We must."

The tone of finality in his voice cut through all their doubts. Even Alphonse, who had been ready to run the entire convoluted path home, felt himself yield, his legs already growing heavy with the task ahead.

Samuel, who had not tasted the flesh, who had only passed his blood-dampened hand across his hot brow, became more and more convinced that even that simple gesture had visited him with madness. The language inside his head was no longer his own. He thought of the fabled sea, and the phrase *mare clausum* rose up on his tongue. When he held the girl—and being the largest of the men, the task fell often to him—he felt . . . he felt . . . struggling for the word to describe his clenched heart, his mind released another unknown word, *miscordia.* Samuel looked over the ragtag group of men, himself included, and thought ruefully: *fortuna favet fortibus*. Hardly realizing how easily he had translated his inner observation, he continued muttering.

But we are cowards, he pleaded, as if offering a reasonable response to the foreigner within him.

A few days after Samuel and the traveling party had departed the village, another stranger arrived in the square. The villagers were puzzled. They had thought the gypsy woman with her map had been the last. A few groused, openly questioning the young man's authenticity. And he *was* different. The other visitors had been entranced by their displays, but this young messenger seemed exhausted and preoccupied as if he'd been chased to the village and might yet be pursued. In the square, he hardly waited for a crowd to gather before he unrolled his exhibit, wrapped in that same odd cloth.

Along with everyone else Flavia had gone to see the other revelations, and, while she had been thrilled by every one, a wonderful confusion came over her at the sight of this young man's display. At first she thought he struggled with a rare animal, but his prize, a speckled band, was more of an event than an object. When he lifted the speckled band tentatively (high above his head so that all could see), the sky grew still, the clouds ceased their wandering and waxed luminous with expectation. Even the raucous sea birds fell silent.

What were they to make of this? In the past the villagers had elbowed forward, wanting a closer look. Now no one moved and the visitor had no time for them anyway. By the time the world regained itself, the young man had the speckled band wrapped again, and he was striding away.

That night Flavia, roaming, came across him as he slept in a gardener's hut by the abandoned river estate. He was a boy really, his hair a shock of silk and his face not yet parched from months at sea. He slept with his young lush mouth open, his new man's arms embracing the bundle. Flavia reached her hand out to touch the boy's bundle, but stopped herself midway and instead lay down in the dust and straw facing him. Improbably, he reached for her in his sleep, and they held each other close, his bundle awkward between them. How long they slept Flavia wasn't sure. When she awakened, the gritty square of window in the gardener's hut was still the color of pitch and the boy was gone. She could hear the river calling as it swept past. For a change, the sound was more plaintive than enticing. She burrowed into the nest they'd made, searching for the stranger's spicy scent, but finding all trace gone she bound up her hair and wandered home.

Early the next morning her sister Josie had a rare adventure of her own. Coming back from the pasture where she'd left Rita, she heard the thud of a shovel meeting dirt. Josie's eyes had only a moment's trouble discerning a young man digging a hole under the huge black walnut tree that marked the way to the river. Her breath stopped—it purely ceased—and her legs rooted themselves to the path as the young man raised his head and, still clasping the shovel loosely, came to meet her.

"The earth is very hard," he said once he was within arm's reach. "I can't make much of a hole here. Maybe you wouldn't mind helping me."

He seemed not to notice her great fear. He stepped closer.

"I am not clever. Digging at this time of year," he went on, "was probably not the best idea, but how else could I leave it? Please." He held out his bundle. "It's very valuable, that's all I know."

"But you were burying it?" Josie said as her hands, trained for helping, reached out involuntarily. She hugged the foreign cloth to her chest.

"It is not mine," the young man said as if that fact explained everything.

"The riverbank," she said suddenly, surprising herself. "The ground is soft there."

He shook his head. "I haven't time. Please, you do it." He looked so young and ordinary now, like one of the cannery boys, and the bundle felt reassuringly solid in her arms, as if, perversely, he had given her protection against him.

"Which way," he asked her, "out of town?"

She pointed, he left, and Josie, emboldened by her escape and the widening shafts of morning light, picked up the boy's shovel and crept toward the river, the treasure cradled in her arms.

When they reached the edge of the village the men hesitated. No one desired to be seen by his family bearing a nearly dead girl as the only prize. Better to arrive empty-handed, to declare the journey a failure, the closed sea a clever myth. Only the question of the girl remained. The girl with her brilliant, mutilated legs. Of course she fell to Samuel in the end, as they knew she would. After all, he had no wife to question his reason, yet his daughters could look after her.

His daughters.

With Josie's help Samuel removed the makeshift bandages and cleaned the girl's legs. Josie's hands trembled, but the sick girl's exquisite stillness reassured her, and she became a steady nurse.

As the weeks passed most of the men recovered. Thoughts of the closed sea and hopes for riches faded away as they actively sought to forget what they had seen and tasted. Their fear and the wretched state in which they'd arrived back on their doorsteps served to clear away the fog of longing that had overcome the village at the arrival of the first messenger. Since they'd returned, the only newcomers to town were a pair of foreigners who identified themselves as fish buyers.

At Samuel's house the girl clung to life. Josie took charge and Flavia, wild Flavia, looked on with awe at her gentle sister's capable nursing. She eagerly ran errands, fetching restoratives—a flask of river water, comfrey from the patch below the pasture. The two of them kept such a dedicated vigil over the patient that Samuel finally acknowledged his exhaustion and began again to sleep nights, reassured that both his girls were within the sound of his voice. Each day the fishgirl grew stronger, and his daughters seemed safer. Not one man talked. Samuel himself silently rejoiced, oblivious for the moment to other changes in town.

* * *

The fish buyers had come, they said, from the capital city. One of the men was a restaurateur whose clientele included the wealthiest, most fashionable citizens of the country. The other claimed to be a simple merchant. They were undeterred by the weather, seemed not to care that they'd arrived in the wrong season, that it would be months before the boats left dock. Together they rented two of the four available rooms at the Whistling Oyster Hotel where they waited, playing hand after hand of a complicated card game they called Devil's Jest. Although several men, Alphonse among them, were invited to join in, not one could get the hang of the game, and most of them drifted away, leaving the two to their often fierce competition.

Then surprise! Scarcely two weeks after the men's return, the weather lost its nerve and a false spring arrived complete with warm breezes and clear skies. With the boats ready, a few made trips out, expecting nothing more than a day's jaunt in the open air. None of the usual fish runs began this early. But for the hell of it Alphonse let his net drop just to see what he might find. The weight of it dismayed him; he was certain he'd picked up debris that would rip his new net to shreds and all before the real season began! Instead he discovered he'd gained a huge load of misshapen crabs streaked with faint blue and lavender markings.

The two city men—the Buyers they came to be called—had wandered down to the dock just as Alphonse eased his boat into its mooring. They could see his piled deck, Alphonse in his high black boots wading through a writhing mass with a rake, and they could barely contain their excitement. They shouted out to Alphonse who could not hear them. But the other fishermen could, and one by one they ceased their tinkering and came to stand on the dock and stare with the Buyers toward Alphonse.

The Buyers went mad for the crabs. Tense and white on the dock, they examined Alphonse's catch, chuckling with pleasure over the thin shells. To the astonishment of the onlookers, the merchant broke a piece of shell and placed it on his tongue, closing his eyes and sighing deeply. Of course the villagers had to try them too—at least the intrepid ones. Alphonse spat the shell out as it began its fizzing melt on his tongue while the Buyers laughed. For others the shell dissolved with a horrid tang, staining their mouths a dirty purple and fouling their breath. Even the meat, gray and oily, tasted repugnant to them. Poison crabs the villagers called them. Alphonse threw up for two days.

"Just as well," the Buyers said, "that you don't develop a taste. You'd devour your profits."

And what profits! The value of a single day's take soon matched what had been last year's entire salary for an average family. The Buyers' customers in the capital delighted in the crab's unusual color and taste.

"It's said," Clive informed the other fisherman, "that these particular crabs contain not poison, but a powerful aphrodisiac. It will be the making of our village."

Overcome by wealth a few village families went wild. Old Claude with his silly young wife, Manda, went so far as to clear a spot by the river, intending an estate grander than the abandoned one. And Alphonse commissioned an entire new wardrobe from the village tailor. Peter the singer did his part by writing a ballad wherein Alphonse appeared as a village hero. The tune was so catchy, so sweetly memorable as performed by Peter, that everywhere one went someone was sure to be humming the chorus.

Unlike the others Samuel stayed home, waiting for the true fishing season. He could not explain exactly why he waited. He was eager to be at sea again, but he was reluctant to leave his girls alone, as much for his sake as for theirs.

Non compos mentis, he said to himself. *I am not of sound mind.*

He saw treachery and danger in the slightest events. An old friend of his wife's peered in his front window, and taking her for an intruder Samuel brandished a stick of firewood and chased her to the edge of the road before he discovered his mistake and called out apologies to her retreating figure. Alphonse came to borrow a spare net, and the young man's face appeared to grow thin as a weasel's before Samuel's eyes. He would not let Alphonse past the front door, but over Samuel's broad shoulder Alphonse spied Flavia as she passed through the sitting room.

"Is that—?" he said craning his neck, his eyes flecked with forgetfulness and more—a growing, uncharacteristic lasciviousness.

"Flavia, my eldest," Samuel said, thinking *anguis in herba—you snake-in-the-grass.*

"The net," he told him with a nudge, "is in the boatshed."

As for Flavia, she would not leave the house now. She hovered by the fishgirl's bed, plying her with dishes of stewed fruit. The fishgirl's eyes, wide and gold-shot, mesmerized her, and she found herself telling the silent girl stories of the river, the dark woods, a boy with a band of moonlight. Flavia's tales were so alluring that Josie began to wonder what she had been missing. Finally Josie screwed up her courage and offered to get the river water herself, long after their father had retired for the night.

At first her heart beat painfully and the muscles in her legs ached. She walked in circles, peering through the dark woods, stopping often to listen. The chatter of the river unnerved her further by obscuring every other hidden sound. Josie raced home that first night and the second—all through a week—but gradually she became used to being out in the night and indeed began to feel protected beneath the embrace of woods and dark.

Alone. Why had no one ever told her how beautiful the night could be? Josie knew the thickened blind of predawn, how it crept away like the tides and allowed the day to emerge. Now she felt the weight of light and how its absence sweetened the unkempt ruins by the river. She learned how the world grows plump and vague when silence descends. Scents meanwhile sharpened so that Josie often found herself standing with her nose in the air, mesmerized by the heady smells of damp moss and tree lichen, the spice of devil's claw, the thin intoxication of salmon-colored trilliums. And yet she was not alone. Under a white river rock, secured with a bit of her father's fishing line, Josie had hidden the bundle she'd been given. Each time she passed this way, she could feel its gentle vibration and was not sure whether she was its caretaker or if the bundle were hers. She wanted very much to show it to someone, to her father or to Flavia. But Flavia would not leave the fishgirl, and her father . . . she had caught him sleeping in his chair the other night, and the look on his face when she'd awakened him had chilled her. He had fingered her jacket, cold and damp from her excursion, with tears in his eyes, but whether they were of relief or happiness or despair Josie was not sure.

In the true spring the real runs began again, but most of the fishermen ignored them for the crabs. The Buyers had no use, they said, for common sprats or haddock. They too were growing ridiculously rich.

Samuel was relieved to be back on his boat, despite the lack of company. A thread of unease remained, but, buoyed up by the fresh weather and the thought of being back on the water, he elected for once to ignore it.

Then in early June the crabs began to disappear. The restaurateur, used to the flux of seasons, returned to the capital. The other Buyer, the older merchant, sought out Alphonse. This man's name was too complicated for the villagers' tongues; among themselves they labeled him *Cashpockets* or *Lord Crab*. To his face they called him *Mister*, while he in turn called them by their Christian names as if he'd known each of them intimately from childhood.

"You were the first, Alphonse," he said, "and I have faith in you. The crabs—how marvelous they were—but if they're gone, they're gone. What's next, I ask you? What thrill can I offer my customers? Can you tell me this?"

Alphonse was dumbfounded, overcome by the Buyer's deference to his expertise. His chest swelled and he grinned, but he had nothing to say. The Buyer waited—he had experience baiting recalcitrant men—and Alphonse did not disappoint. Before minutes had passed he was babbling.

"Ask Clive," he said finally, "and Peter, old Claude—they'll tell you."

When Samuel arrived back at the harbor the next evening, all was quiet. Only a few of the fishermen milled around their decks. The rest had no need to go out. Rich men they were now, a town of rich men. On the deserted dock the Buyer was waiting for Samuel. He kept his hands folded neatly on his vest as he observed Samuel go through the multitude of chores that signaled the end of his workday: unloading his catch for the cannery boy, washing down the deck, coiling the ropes and winding the nets back in place. Finally as Samuel lumbered up the dock the Buyer fell in step beside him as if they were old friends, saying nothing until they'd passed through the warren of town streets and embarked on the road that led to Samuel's cottage.

"You're an odd one, Samuel, turning down the crab. But maybe you don't need riches, eh? Maybe you're the wealthiest of them all?"

Samuel snorted.

"Maybe you went on a journey and came home with the golden pot, left the others empty-handed, eh?"

Samuel felt his fists clench.

The Buyer must have noticed. His voice altered, taking on a more conciliatory tone. "Of course you couldn't have known. It was you who was saddled with . . . what shall we call it . . . *lusus naturae?*"

"No freak of nature," Samuel found himself saying, "only *ignotium*—the unknown one."

"I can take her away. You will be free of all responsibility."

Later Samuel would try to reconstruct this conversation without success. He would wonder at how easily they'd understood each other, but, at the moment, he slid easily into the language of his private thoughts.

"Cui bono?" Samuel queried, imagining Flavia's face if this man arrived at their door.

The Buyer grew impatient. "You understand me," he said to Samuel. "She is in your head making you mad, is she not? She leads you to a path of destruction. And then there is the matter of a murdered man. Oh, Samuel, what hope can you have with her there always reminding you of what might have been? You, a righteous man!"

Samuel's head momentarily filled with bees. The confusion of the last months, his household inverted. Last night he had awakened at a sound in the garden and peering out had spied Josie striding up the path from the river. Now Samuel shook his head.

"Dum spiro, spero," he told the Buyer.

"While you breathe, indeed!" the Buyer sneered, losing his usual composure. They had reached Samuel's house. Ahead of them, in the window, Flavia's bright head appeared momentarily. Samuel stopped to light his pipe, but the Buyer wasn't fooled.

"Ah, yes, the daughter." He rubbed a greasy hand over his well-shaved cheek. "I've heard of her, the would-be mermaid."

Samuel left the leering Buyer in the lane. His heart hammering, he threw the bolt on the door. Josie stirred a pot of soup; Flavia soaked bandages in river water. Samuel barely restrained himself from rushing to them, drawing them under his huge embrace. His daughters did not notice his agitation but kept to their tasks. Only the apricot-skinned girl, curled in his armchair, met his eyes—and eased his heart.

* * *

At the river's edge Josie leads her father to the buried bundle. Flavia removes the fishgirl's bandages, marveling at the beauty of her healed legs. No moment exists for thanks. For who owes gratitude to whom? Josie hands over the speckled band, and the fishgirl takes it with the slightest of smiles, handing the rough blanket back without a word. The sound of a single girl slipping into water is a mere rustle, but a shudder of joy runs through Samuel and his daughters as they stand close together on the riverbank. The moon lights a clean path straight up the river, and they watch and watch until the night returns to normal. A few stars. A tree creaking in the wind.

In his warm room at the Whistling Oyster, the Buyer hears the echo of a splash and, looking up from his cards, lets loose a cry of frustration and throws his hands up before his face. Alphonse, whom he has been beating badly, takes the opportunity to snatch the Queen of Spades from the deck and place it on his own pile of cards to win the hand. He is wearing a ridiculous cream-colored suit with a pair of shiny beige shoes, already heavily scratched from the cobbled village streets, and while he waits for the Buyer to acknowledge his remarkable feat Alphonse pretends he is a man of refined sensibilities. He sips at the thick foreign wine in his glass and smacks his lips in a pretense of enjoyment, oblivious to the window beside him and the night sky where a ripple of moonlight wends its way through the clouds as if tightening a seam around the earth.

HEARTSICK

HE WAS AN EVIL, AWFUL MAN AND THE CAT HAD NEVER liked him. Sprawled on the kitchen tablecloth, morning sunshine purling his gray fur, the cat had never grown used to the hiss of Mulligan's voice, the rough hand on his neck, the cold, enforced leap into the dew-drenched backyard. At night, with his claws only partly retracted, the cat practiced springing onto the bed, targeting the man's shorts or the tender underside of his throat. Once when he'd been going through the change from kitten to tom he sprayed the inside of the man's closet. He paid for that of course, with a nasty visit to the vet that he pretended to forget a lot sooner than he actually had.

During the summer after the boy left, the cat dug auger-shaped holes in the majestic pots of fuchsias beside the swimming pool and squatted over them intently before scattering potting soil and bits of his own creamy turds into the shallow end where Mulligan liked to soak.

When winter came and a tissue of ice began to form on the slate walkway leading up to the house, the cat practiced scratching at the French door, the one with the faulty latch, until he perfected the midnight feat of opening the door a good six inches, enough to allow the first snow to make a damp nest on the living room's hardwood floor.

In retaliation Mulligan bought, from a wholesale grocery store (he was cheap too), cases of an unlabeled brand of food that the cat naturally refused. When Mulligan declared the beast must eat what he was fed or starve, the cat complied, eating heartily each morning and throwing up every afternoon on the Oriental runner, on the papers on Mulligan's desk, in his golfing shoes. When Mulligan reduced his portions the cat took to hunting, leaving the bloodied remains of a neighbor's carrier pigeon to stain Mulligan's newspaper as it lay unprotected on the front doorstep.

Oh, there were scenes. There were standoffs. At the vet's Mulligan feigned concern, reaching out to take the cat from the embrace of the gentle girl who assisted the vet in his exam. The cat hissed at his touch. *I know who you are*, the cat said to Mulligan, *even if they don't.*

But despite all his transgressions the cat could not be let go. He had been beloved by Mulligan's son, Vance, and so claimed an inviolable place in Mulligan's household. The two were bound together, trussed hand and foot by that love, and neither could break the bond.

Ten months earlier, on a rainy spring morning when other students were finishing up exams, Mulligan's sixteen-year-old son had caught a bus to Hartford. There he purchased a ticket (on the credit card Mulligan had given him for emergencies) to Santa Fe, New Mexico, via Atlanta. The credit card had surfaced a month later at an outdoor equipment store in Seattle. Mulligan still carried the receipt bearing Vance's distinctive scrawl in his wallet. Tonight as he paced the hallway in front of Vance's quiet room he hunted for it between his own credit cards, using the weak shaft of light from the hall to read again the list of items: a two-man Eureka tent, a folding backpacking stove, and a plastic egg protector. After that last charge in June there had been nothing else. The detective Mulligan and his wife Susan hired to augment the almost nonexistent police search was puzzled by Vance's limited use of the credit card.

"Sometimes it takes a year or more," he informed an agonized Susan, "but kids like Vance aren't all that hard to find. They're used to high living. Creature comforts. They use the card. We find them."

He suggested Mulligan report the card as stolen to alert shopkeepers who would hold Vance for the police, but months went by and still there was nothing.

"Confidentially," the detective told Mulligan when they were alone, "the drug connection makes everything more difficult. Logic flies out the window. A kid will do anything when drugs are involved."

"It wasn't Vance," Mulligan said coldly. "His friends. The wrong crowd. He's a terrifically loyal friend."

The detective had looked away then, merely

nodded at Mulligan with much the same look that Mulligan now offered his son's cat, who appeared at the far end of the hallway sidling into Vance's room.

At first Susan hardly went out. She wanted to be by the phone. She never blamed him. The days of bitter arguments had ended with Vance's departure. Neither of them had the energy. Vance's birthday passed, the start of a new school year, the awful round of holidays. Susan fell to pieces in November. For days she would not get out of bed. A stone-faced Mulligan drove her to a doctor, filled her prescriptions. Then a classmate of Vance's died in an "accident" in his parents' garage, a note pinned to his shirt.

"Like Paddington," Susan said. "Remember how Vanny loved that part: *Please take care of this bear*."

Only *that* boy's note had spewed invectives at his socialite mother and shyster dad. Susan rose from her darkened room to befriend the mother, and in no time a support group was formed. Mulligan watched as Susan floated back up to the surface, while he sank noiselessly to the bottom of his own grief. He was left with a file on his son, complete with dental records, that he carted around in his briefcase, and an unreasonable hatred for the cat who was still there, always waiting for Mulligan to do the right thing and return his boy. From the hallway he could hear the thin rasp of the cat's snore. Mulligan slipped inside the room. He reached over and lifted the edge of his son's pillow where the cat slept, making a steep ledge that the creature easily slipped off.

"Out," Mulligan said as the cat landed with a skittering thud on the rug. "Shoo."

He was, of course, not an ordinary cat at all, but a *trained* cat with a bag of well chosen and self-satisfying tricks. There were maybe two or three other cats in the whole country with his talent, Vance had whispered to him once, and they lived in Kansas or Mississippi where there was little opportunity for advancement. Vance's cat could commute to New York City if the occasion arose. Vance had taught him to fetch balls made of aluminum foil. Well, maybe not *taught.* Vance had *facilitated* the cat's skills. They were partners. Vance had read somewhere that the aluminum foil sent low levels of electrical current through the cat's teeth into his brain, a sensation that was both pleasurable and addictive. And did the cat appreciate Vance's new information? Almost certainly. Every night they practiced in the treehouse Vance had built at the far edge of Mulligan's property. Fetching, leaping into the air for a catch, gathering a multitude of shiny balls into one glittering pile on the treehouse floor before scattering them again with a well aimed swipe. The cat was pure genius.

It was Vance who had discovered the cat's most wonderful skill. When he was torn by anger or a deep, unnameable sadness, the boy would call the cat to him, cradle him in his arms, and begin the stroking that would transfer painful emotion to the cat, who absorbed Vance's cares willingly. For what place can anxiety or despair or love gone wrong claim within the soul of a cat? Vance had once done a report on human skin and had learned how certain noxious substances became benign when passed through the upper layers of the derma. That was what it was like with the cat. Rage and heartsickness would slowly leave Vance when he held the cat. He would be left empty and healed, his sweetest daydreams slowly arriving. Afterward the cat would sit in the corner for a half-hour washing himself thoroughly before returning, purring, to the boy's side. The two of them would lean back in the sagging couch in Vance's treehouse and rest peacefully together.

Ah, if Mulligan had only known.

Since Vance's departure Mulligan thought he'd grown used to being tired, but now it seemed all the punch had gone out of him. Lassitude sat on his shoulders, pressed its palms against his eyes, and sent him stumbling heavily through his days. He had never been so ridiculously weary.

Nothing seemed to rouse him. He woke up exhausted and wavered over the washbasin, trying to shave, feeling as if his bones had gone to jelly and he was being shrugged off the frame of his being. Driving to work one morning his hands slipped off the steering wheel momentarily, and he nearly jumped a curb, terrifying a clutch of high-school girls. Once they recovered they shot him the finger in unison.

"Maybe I have mono," he said to Susan when he

called for their morning check-in. No news, as usual.

"Don't you get that from kissing?" she asked him. "Hours and hours of making out."

He closed his eyes, hesitated, but said it anyway. "Well, I didn't get it from you then."

After another pause Susan answered him. "You're right there, Gerry."

He got worse. Forty-six years old and he couldn't climb the stairs without holding the rail. In the corporate offices where he worked as a controller (a glorified accountant, Susan called him once during a vicious argument), his decline did not go unnoticed. He cut back on business trips and spent whole weekends in his big leather chair, unable even to spar with the cat who lay habitually now on the kitchen counter, taunting him.

Yet tired as he was, Mulligan wasn't sleeping well, and he and the cat had entered into an uneasy alliance, sharing the desolate quiet of a house at night. This had been Vance's time. Mulligan could remember awakening long after the boy's curfew to hear the refrigerator door snap open or the television scan forward in a startling volley of musical snatches and voice fragments.

Now, following his son's pattern, Mulligan claimed the night. The cat noticed and cautiously approved the change. Sometimes he even came close to vaulting into Mulligan's lap, but a swift glance told him those other nocturnal leaps had not been forgotten. Restless, Mulligan wandered from room to room. From the doorway of his own bedroom he regarded

Susan enviously as she slept openmouthed. He leaned against the sink in the kitchen and filled a glass with cloudy tap water, then waited for it to clear before taking the few sips that never failed to nauseate him. In the dark of the living room he gazed out the French doors. If he stood there long enough, and there was still snow on the ground to reflect the moon's light, he could see past the outline of the pool to Vance's treehouse and, beyond that, the roofline of the newly formed Sandalwood School. Tears gathered in his eyes as he leaned against the glass doors. The cat tucked himself on the footstool beside the fireplace and pretended not to notice.

One exceptionally dismal February morning Mulligan awakened in the leather chair in his den where he'd finally collapsed. Susan had already left. It was how they managed these days, avoiding each other under the pretense of errands and work. Saturday morning: Susan's weekly hair appointment followed by coffee with the support group. Outside his study window the sky was a hard sheet of blue ice. Mulligan forced himself to dress in layers of warm clothes topped off by Vance's old winter coat, an overlarge green down jacket. As he enfolded himself in the jacket the mantra returned—*Where are you? Where are you?* The first rainy night after they knew Vance was gone, Susan had stood at the window watching the far-off flash of lightning. "Where *are* you, Vance?" she'd said over and over, each word clipped and sharpened by hysteria.

From the moment he entered the woods, leaves swirled toward Mulligan, nicking his face. He hunched down into the coat, his neck going stiff with the effort. Check the treehouse, he told himself, then back to the warm chair, but he was too weary to climb the treehouse ladder and instead sank onto a rock by the creek that marked the edge of his property. Meanwhile the cat scratched at the ghostly trunk of a nearby beech tree. The sound, so like one he had heard on his dining room chairs, inspired Mulligan to make a meager but icy snowball. His weak throw hit its mark and the cat shot away. Faintly elated, Mulligan returned to his meditation on the creek, which was full of copper-colored pebbles and, here and there, flat gray rocks that turned white in the afternoon sunshine.

It didn't take long for Mulligan to realize that something was wrong. The flow of the stream had nearly stopped. He dragged himself toward the frigid water, and found a dam of Rolling Rock bottles held together with nylon thread. More crisscrossing threads were tethered to tree branches on each side of the creek. Several of the bottles were cracked, even broken. Within a few seconds Mulligan found Vance's Swiss Army knife in his pocket, cut the threads on his side of the stream, and, balancing on the rock, crossed the narrow channel to do the same on the other side.

The cat observed his lumbering moves from behind a tree. Just as Mulligan yanked the string of bottles from the water, the cat dashed across the rocks and between the man's legs. Startled, Mulligan jerked his hand back fiercely. The line of bottles swung around, and one of the broken ones caught him on the side of his hand, leaving a neat red gash that swiftly took on a life of its own, drenching the cuff of his shirt.

Mulligan, his hand numb from the water, felt no pain whatsoever. Instead, for the first time in weeks, he experienced a renewed energy. He pulled his shirt-sleeve and the cuff of Vance's jacket over his wound and clutched it tightly against his stomach. The cat had halted on a bare patch of earth under a tree. Mulligan formally cursed him, shaking the bottles in the direction of the furred ridge of the cat's back. Still the cat pretended to ignore him. He sauntered up the path toward the Sandalwood School, and Mulligan, after a moment's hesitation, resolved to follow him there. If he didn't make a stand now, they'd overrun the place. Violation—just what Vance had felt when Mulligan had directed the police to the treehouse. Violation and betrayal. He could not have guessed that they would find a box stuffed with bags of pot, neat zip-locks that did not, of course, belong to Vance. They said they only wanted to talk to the boy about a friend of his. And if Mulligan had known? He glanced back at the silent treehouse, hidden by the camouflage of its gray weathered boards, and felt a familiar moment of panic.

The Sandalwood School was ridiculously small, nothing at all like the school where Mulligan and Susan had sent Vance after the arrest. The campus of Vance's school was rich with stone buildings named after benefactors. There was a chapel larger than the Episcopal church in the nearby town, and a science building designed and staffed by graduates from MIT. The students wore simple uniforms—blazers and ties—and said, "Good morning, sir," when Mulligan passed them on the grounds. Despite the months of futile searching preceded by the awful day when he'd gone to collect Vance's belongings, Mulligan still thought of his son at that school, so diligent, so happy he'd simply forgotten to call home.

In contrast the Sandalwood School had emerged from probate court. A distant cousin of Leon Whittaker had inherited the remnants of that alcoholic's estate. As he picked his way over the dirty traces of last week's snowstorm Mulligan dodged pieces of trash and a continual trail of dog shit that ended up at a wide decaying porch where the cat hopped on a railing as if he owned the place. Several students dressed in tattered clothing sprawled around rusting café tables on the porch, smoking cigarettes. Mulligan had a fleeting impression of deformity: irregularly shaped heads, faces marked by piercings and pox, a tattooed hand. A girl in a floor-length fur coat wove in front of him, holding a video camera up to her face, filming his ascent to the building.

By the time Mulligan had made it up the stairs and into the school's front hall he felt himself sinking. Standing in the once elegant entryway, recoiling from the strange musk smell that seemed to emanate from the walls, he almost bailed. Groups of children always made him uneasy, recalling his own tortured youth. He had lied to Vance continually through the boy's childhood. Over and over Vance had begged Mulligan to repeat his favorite stories about Mulligan's adventures with his Maine cousins. Vance didn't seem to notice the inconsistencies until he was fourteen and an apprentice cynic. *If you were so close to these cousins,* he asked Mulligan, *why don't they ever visit? Why don't we ever go to Maine and sail in their little boat?*

"Goliath! Goliath!" a girl's voice yelled impatiently from the porch.

A towheaded boy, no older than five, appeared at the head of the stairs in front of Mulligan. As he raced past, Mulligan half shouted for directions to the school's office, which the boy gave with surprising cheeriness and lucidity.

Mulligan followed a short flight of stairs down to an old service room. Behind the secretary's desk, a young woman with black-rimmed eyes and a thick smear of orange lipstick looked up expectantly. Mulligan made her wait while he found a place to sit in the cluttered office and caught his breath. Finally he began the tirade that to his own disgust came out cautiously mild. His traitorous voice, congested from his climb up the cold hill, whined. The secretary smiled—condescendingly, Mulligan thought—throughout his speech and then, in the gentlest of manners, assured him that the bottles were not the result of a party on his property but an integral aspect of an environmental experiment.

"See," she told him pointing to a grid of white lines carelessly painted on the side of the bottle he'd deposited on her desk, "these are to measure levels. Or they were. I suppose the class will have to start all over again." She spoke slowly and carefully with a trace of rebuke in her voice.

He was sweating under the weight of Vance's jacket. The warmth of the building brought his injury to life. The cut on his hand throbbed heavily like a small dangerous animal, and he clutched his sleeve tighter, holding his hand to his chest as if he were about to take an oath. He decided to let the incident go with a vague threat of litigation that flew right over the young secretary's head.

When she still smiled down on him, flecks of orange on her teeth, Mulligan found himself saying, "What the hell kind of name is Sandalwood anyway? It sounds like a racetrack."

"Oooh, wait," she said to him as if he were about to spring out the door. She rummaged in a desk drawer and brought out a piece of brown wire and a small vial. She lit a match and a thick curl of smoke streamed from the piece of wire, filling the air with a sweetish smell that identified for Mulligan the source of the odor in the hall.

"And here," the secretary said reaching out toward him. Before he could stop her she'd drizzled some oil from her vial onto his good hand.

"Go ahead," she said, "rub it in and take a good whiff."

Mulligan didn't need to. The smell had shot through his system. It permeated his nostrils; he could taste it on his tongue.

"Sandalwood is an anointing oil," the girl said, again unbearably slowly. "Buddhists use it in funeral rites, to help speed the soul on to its new life. That's kind of our metaphor here, you know: the kids moving on to new lives."

The smoke, now pip-piping off the wire, heavy with scent, was making Mulligan nauseous. He closed his eyes for a moment, gathering his strength, just as a blast of what sounded like gunshots resounded from somewhere above them.

"Pigeon containment," the secretary said hopping up cheerfully. "Our fourth floor is overrun."

"You're shooting them?" Mulligan said. "Here? Upstairs?"

"They're using an improvised blowgun," she explained in that annoyingly deliberate voice. "It stuns the birds and then the boys scoop 'em up and move 'em out. One of Gil Bevis's inventions. He's such an amazing kid."

"Surely there's an ordinance against that sort of thing," Mulligan said, but the secretary wasn't listening. A weaselly-looking child—boy or girl, Mulligan couldn't tell—with a shaved head the shape of a thumb rushed into the office and began rifling through the secretary's desk drawers, shouting, "Staples, Mary Ann! Gil says we need staples!" The secretary, after handing over a box, astonished Mulligan by rushing out behind the child, giggling and demanding to know the "count."

"Nice to meet you, neighbor," she shouted back to Mulligan as an afterthought.

Anxious to be home, he stood to leave. Already he could imagine the sweet relief of his bed. The events of the recent past dissolved, and he let himself feel Susan laying him down, stroking his hair; Susan coming unbidden to lie beside him. How they would sleep! Through years of squabbling and misunderstanding, through one full dark week and all these months of loss.

But Mulligan couldn't move. His arms tingled. Inside his chest his heart shuddered and twisted like a heavy stone held aloft with the thinnest of ropes. The air in front of him shimmied, and through it the green bottle he'd placed on the secretary's desk began a wavering, black-edged dance. Beyond it, in the corner of the room, a patch of bare carpet beckoned. Mulligan slid to the floor and crawled. His head found a tottering stack of videotapes. He drew his legs up and let himself bob and weave, finally disappearing under a great wave of weariness. Off in the distance, high above his head, cheering broke out. From the depths of his fatigue Mulligan murmured, "Good boy, Vanny. Well done."

The girl with the camcorder—her name was Linnea D'Braesio—found Mulligan. She'd only been out of juvie a week, was still on probation for giving her step-mother, Nonie, a broken nose, and her first instinct was to run. She could imagine a dozen ways the man in the corner might harm her. Her worst fear was soon calmed: he wasn't dead. He was making a god-awful sound, something between a wheeze and a high nasal snore, but he looked cozy despite his awkward position. The contradiction appealed to her just as her first sight of him with his thin, chiseled face and bulky green jacket had struck her filmmaker's interest. The noise, however, was unbearable, and the man was so pale that Linnea could see a sharp raw ridge forming along his cheek from where it rested on the videotapes.

Man, she whispered to him, what did you do to deserve this?

The secretary, Mary Ann, had left the vial of sandalwood oil out on her desk and Linnea spotted it. One of the other kids, Dahl or Lydia, had told her that the oil had special powers. It cleared away bad energy or attracted new spirits, she wasn't entirely sure. So far it hadn't done much for her. Or for the others. Dahl was in a daze most of the time, and Lydia was still stuck with her kid. (Imagine, Linnea thought, having a kid when you were twelve-and-a-half.) But what the hell, she thought, it can't do any harm. She emptied the vial over Mulligan. Then, because it seemed the right thing to do, she pressed the record button and edged closer, taping steadily until Mary Ann came back with Gil. It was Gil who said they'd better call an ambulance. Linnea got some excellent footage of the ambulance's arrival, the man's bloodied hand a revelation on the white sheet of the stretcher. What was almost as good were the faces of her fellow students. It was as if they were all on that stretcher or were somehow responsible. Linnea knew that some of them, like Dahl, had been carted off themselves once or twice. They frowned at her as she pushed her way closer to the ambulance. "Gross," she heard someone say. Then, "Don't be morbid or anything, D'Braesio."

Linnea wanted to bang her camcorder over whoever had said that. What the hell did they know about what she was trying to do? Just as she raised the camcorder in her hand she felt a reassuring pressure against her leg and looked down to find that cat twining through her legs.

For an entire afternoon her Environmental Ed class had camped out by the river, taking samples and building the dam. They'd eaten lunch there and sipped hot chai from a thermos while they'd listened to Gil Bevis explain his project, but none of them, not even the fabulous Gil, had thought to look up. As they were leaving, Linnea turned to chuck a rock against the bottles, and there was the cat suspended on a wide branch above her. The branch gradually came into focus as the treehouse's platform. It was his stance, defiantly lonely, that drew her instantly, and when (after waiting for the others to leave) she entered the treehouse for the first time he had fairly raced to greet her, purring loudly as if he had been waiting and waiting, and finally she had arrived.

Now, standing in the school driveway surrounded

by her enemies, Linnea crouched and the cat came to her again. He snuggled close and she ran her hands with their torn nails and bitten down cuticles across his fur over and over again. As her heart calmed and the ambulance drove away, she glanced around at her classmates with sudden affection.

"Hey," she said shyly, approaching the circle around Gil Bevis. "Anyone up for a party?" The cat nestled against her fur coat. "I know this place . . ." she began.

A bad heart knows no recourse. Call it dropsy, call it cardiomyopathy, call it the wicked infidelity of what should have been the most faithful of organs. If the cat had heard the diagnosis he might have felt a peculiar satisfaction. He had known it all along it seemed.

The doctors sent Mulligan home. He was a dead man. No, worse, a ghoul lying in wait for a dead man. Sooner or later someone would die. Maybe Mulligan. Maybe some hotshot teenager with a heart pumped full of lust and hope would miss the turn on his motorcycle ("donorcycles" they called them at the hospital), and Mulligan would be reborn with the heart of a child. For now, he could hardly move.

"Choose your room," Susan told him when she brought him home, "and we'll get you settled."

Mulligan looked warily around for the cat as he stepped into the front hall. It would be like him to mount an attack when Mulligan was at his weakest.

Susan wanted him to camp in the study where his

chair and books were. It would be an easy matter to bring in a bed and television, and the study was close to the kitchen and bath. Also it was a more appropriate place to receive well-wishing visitors. Mulligan, however, didn't expect visitors. He wanted Vance's room with its inconvenient location up still another flight of stairs. Susan wasn't happy about his choice, but, newly tender toward him, she gave in easily.

In the hospital he had lain alone between tests. His colleagues sent flowers by way of their secretaries, but no one visited. He knew he was not a well liked man, but he had never figured out the why of it, just as, when a boy, he had never understood why other children would sidle away from him. He was grieved to feel so abandoned when Susan went home. His best friends were a plastic bowl he filled frequently, and an orderly who called him Buddy and grasped his hand once when he had nearly fainted coming out of the bathroom.

The cat, not to be shut out, jiggled his paw underneath Vance's bedroom door until the latch moved and the door creaked open, but Mulligan did not notice his entrance. He was too busy trying to open the window beside Vance's bed. A light appeared in the woods below. As he eased back into bed he thought he heard music and could almost make out the shifting shadows of dancers.

The cat leaped easily onto the bed, sniffed at the frigid breeze before settling down beside Mulligan's right thigh. The man put his hand on the cat absently, began to stroke. In the dark room Mulligan tensed, his head bent toward the open window. The vague flutter of luminosity in the woods recalled for Mulligan an image from his childhood—sunlight glinting off a bay in northern Maine, an isolated spot where he had spent a summer month with his lesser-known grandmother and a group of cousins who had detested him on sight—the same cousins he had mythologized for Vance. He had been, he could see now, too pushy, too proud. "Let me," he'd say forcefully as they began some new game, and his cousins would pull back and leave him alone.

Lying in Vanny's bed, he remembered a day when he had gone with his grandmother and cousins to a nearby island to collect gulls' eggs. His grandmother used them in her angel food cakes. Only gulls' eggs, she swore, beat up so well. His big grandmother rowed them over in the dory that had been his grandfather's and walked the rocky beach below as Mulligan and his three cousins climbed the stiff face of the bluff to the ledges where the kittiwakes left their eggs. It had seemed to Mulligan like an Easter egg hunt, and while his cousins quietly went about their business he was fired with the spirit of competition. He sharpened his eyes and scrambled over the ledges slick with guano, making terrible growls to offset the shrieks of the kittiwakes. *Angel food.* He'd never heard of such a thing. His mother bought eclairs and petit fours; for his birthday she had the bakery make a decorated sheet cake. Angel's food from gulls' eggs. This was a revelation to Mulligan. He wondered what would happen if he ate one entire egg himself. If he'd rise above the small bratty boy the world knew into something greater, something almost *holy*, or at least likable.

Here was the part of the story he had never told Vance. The next morning after he and his grandmother had gone over to his cousins' house, Mulligan sneaked back to his grandmother's. The stove was still lit from breakfast. He piled more sticks of wood within the little grate just as he'd watched his granny do. He lifted the cast iron pan from its hook above the stove and scooped some bacon grease from the tin cup at the back of the stove before removing his gull egg out of the cup where he'd hidden it. He cracked the egg into a dish, nearly fainting with horror at what he'd exposed. The yolk, instead of the expected golden, was a deep red. The ring around the yolk, normally white, shone a pale green. The mess terrified Mulligan, but what could he do? Already the grease was sizzling, the pan sending up thin streaks of black smoke. Hurriedly he broke the yolk with a fork and scrambled it in the pan. With equal speed he shoved it on a plate and pushed the trembling red mass burning into his mouth, swallowing each bite without chewing. Afterward he bustled around like any housewife, cleaning up his mess, but his stomach, his chest, his throat all loudly complained. Around his mouth he felt a ring of fire as if he'd been marked by the stolen egg. Hours later his cousin Katie found him lying on the slick painted boards of the front porch, his head wedged under the railing as he vomited into the hydrangeas, all chance of redemption gone. Now, remembering, Mulligan felt the familiar tug, and reaching for his bowl he was sick once more.

He shifted in the bed, sore in every part of his body, and drew his son's sweet-smelling blanket around his shoulders, momentarily displacing the cat who rearranged himself under a fold of the blanket. His hand itched under the bandage. Unconsciously Mulligan rubbed it back and forth along the blanket's silken hem, following the lines of the cat beneath. The music rose steeply, and Mulligan, overcome, leaned closer to the window. Vanny was home, he was sure of it.

"Gerry," Susan called from downstairs, "are you all right?"

He could not answer. Instead he pulled the cat closer under his arm, and his sobs quieted, overtaken by the purring of his son's marvelous cat, who was doing the best he could with what the boy had left him.

THE FISHERMAN'S WIFE

DEVON HAD BEEN UP NORTH FOR OVER A MONTH WHEN Lori told me her dream. We sat amid pots of stiff rosemary and frail yellowing basil on the deck that Dev had built to take advantage of the view. Lighthouse Point was below us, there at the rounding of the inlet toward Salish Bay, and beyond, in the distance, we could barely see the outer islands, hazy purple shapes like a gathering of sea creatures perched benignly on the edge of another world. Moments before, the sun had been so direct and warm that I'd been running an ice cube up and down my arm, but now heavy slips of clouds were moving in from the west bringing a sudden chill. I could tell by Lori's wistful expression that she was remembering Dev's April departure—*Little Orca* clattering away through the fog as if she wouldn't make it across the straits let alone up the inland waterway to Ketchikan.

When she had this dream, Lori said, she stopped

breathing and woke up gasping and heaving on the far side of the bed. If Devon was home he made a joke of it, telling her about a sea lion that came up once in the nets. He had to give it artificial respiration. Like this, Dev would say and put his mouth on hers over and over until her heart calmed. I'd be lost without him, Lori said, dead lost. You're lost with him, I wanted to say. It was his life he breathed into her, not hers, and anyone could have predicted that at some point he would snatch it back.

Some days while I'm cleaning fish at the cannery, up to my shins in heads and guts, scenes will appear, some remembered, some imagined, and I find myself back in the company of Lori and Dev. I hear Patrick's voice and Lori turns to me with one of her sudden, surprising smiles. *Suzanne!* they call to me, and we are all friends again. But then the hose ignites with its startling blast in the next bay, or Crazy Cox, the cannery owner, comes screaming out of his office, and I realize that the story I've been telling is just that, an invention. I race along clutching remembered details, drawing conclusions, building rickety scenes on the insubstantial platform of a bystander's memory, wanting to make sense.

It hadn't taken much effort for me to convince Lori to come up to Salish Bay the fall she quit school. I could tell that alone in her dorm room she had slipped into a state of near panic. Whenever Lori grew anxious she could barely speak. I had to strain to hear her whispered story. She had switched majors three times, muddling her transcript with useless courses. She was in so far over her head she could never catch up. Which is why she decided to leave. Bellingham was full of fast-food restaurants, video stores, and espresso carts. She had been sure she'd find some kind of work. But, oh, the job applications! She hadn't reckoned on interviews either—she was in no shape to be questioned. Of course no one ever called her back.

For my part I had lost my roommate. Already I was having trouble paying rent on the ground-floor apartment of one of Salish Bay's shabbier Victorians. I'll admit I was lonely too, tired to death of seeking attachments. The walls of my apartment were saturated with tirades against work and lovers. Recently I'd been able to feel some of my spent venom seeping back into me. Some mornings I woke up and the first thing in my head as I focused on my shabby quilt and the piles of laundry covering my dusty floor was a voice saying *Fuck you.* I needed company, that was plain. Lori and I had an ease together born of mutual humiliations beginning with our first meeting as two rejects from a camp softball game.

Two days after my phone call Lori set off, her battered Subaru stuffed with the remnants of two years of dorm rooms. She drove into town, following a series of steeply inclined blind curves, the last of which opened on a view of Salish Bay.

From the top of the hill Salish Bay must have seemed flawless to Lori. A toy town with peaked roofs scattered behind a main street of handsome brick buildings. The bay in front was a rare blue with white points rising in the breeze. On the far side of town, in the boat haven protected by a stone breakwater, fishing boats were berthed alongside wooden sailboats with the occasional hippie houseboat and Crazy Cox's ferrocement barge thrown in for more local color.

On her way down Buckley Hill, Lori turned into the parking lot of the Salmon Cove Cafe to take in the view. For months when I first came to town I tried to get Karen Clatts, the owner of the café, to hire me. I'd heard that during tourist season a waitress made more in a single night at the café than Crazy Cox was paying for an entire week of fish gutting. But Karen favored pale artsy types for her help, wraiths she could charm and intimidate with her frantic pace and her little earthenware dishes of olive oil. I was too real for her, I think. Thin women are often afraid of other—more womanly—women.

Some sort of pretty plant—gray-leaved with tufts of feathery white blooms—was growing on the edge of the empty parking lot the morning Lori parked her Subaru there. Lori stared at the plant for several minutes before realizing it wasn't a plant at all but a dead and ravaged gull. She was still sitting there five minutes later, squinting her eyes and trying to remake the dead bird into a marvelous shrub, when Karen Clatts banged on her window startling Lori out of her reverie.

Karen began talking the moment Lori got out of the car.

"God," she said, "what a day to be late. Sorry, sorry. I usually schedule more time for training. I'm so glad you got my message. Your phone kept disconnecting me. I wasn't sure I even had the right number. To tell the truth I dropped your application in the sink by accident, and it was a *challenge* to read after that."

She led Lori through the kitchen and into the dining room, pointing out work stations and a numbered chart of tables. She moved too quickly for Lori to tell her she'd made a mistake. In a matter of minutes Lori was hunched over a huge stainless steel sink rinsing lettuce leaves. The afternoon flew by one chore after another. At three-thirty a waitress called in sick, and Karen begged Lori to begin waiting tables today. Lori just nodded. She filled water glasses when patrons arrived, bussed tables, and took orders shyly. She amazed herself with her efficiency. When a woman complained her pumpkin lamb soup was tepid, Lori took it to the kitchen and found the microwave without saying a word. At the end of the evening she collected more than sixty dollars in tips, a draw for which both Karen and the other waitress, Tessa, apologized. Once you know your way around, you'll get more tables, they assured her. They smiled at Lori as she filled out forms and saw her name inked onto the schedule, and Karen herself came to the back door to call out goodnight.

I put my own feelings aside. I did—really. I forgot that I'd already talked to Crazy Cox about a job for Lori and instead told myself that a roommate who could pay her own way was what I'd wanted all along. Celebrate, I told Lori, we must celebrate. It was only natural that Happy Jacks Cardroom came to mind. Happy Jacks may not be the fanciest place in Salish Bay, but its location on the scrubby outskirts of town, tucked on a precipice, gives the bar an extra aura of possibility. Luck was something you grabbed when it was hot, I said, having just been through a rough patch with my now ex-boyfriend. Mine was due for a change. I had this thought that I could win enough for a trip to a Mexican resort. I'd drink icy Pacificos with drifters of a better class than the ones who washed up on the shores of this town. That would piss off a few people wouldn't it, Suzanne in Paradise?

"Hola!" I called out as we entered Happy Jacks.

A few loggers at a half-full table glanced up with what I took to be interest. Their red suspenders and blue-striped shirts made them look like toddlers at a game of Go Fish. My ex had been part of the group who tied themselves to the high limbs of the old growth cedars, defying the loggers to commit multiple murder. I couldn't help feeling a certain amount of affection for these ruddy faced, muscled men. In fact I wish I had a photograph of them in action: the chainsaws humming and my ex and his holier-than-thous bailing out like chickens caught roosting in an old farm truck.

"Hey, Chichita," one of them called to me, waving us over.

The only other patrons at the card tables were a

drunken Dane, Cor Nielsen, whose wife had just left him, and a pair of realtors with thinning hair and paunches. I didn't notice the Lund brothers then, staking out the back table in the dark adjacent bar.

Lori lasted a couple of hands, just watching. She wasn't much of a gambler, and she didn't seem especially pleased with the increasingly bold advances of the loggers. One of them was on a streak. Another kept moving closer and closer until his leg lay against my own. I hardly noticed when Lori drifted off toward the bar. She gave me the details later, a blow by blow description of love at first sight.

Devon Lund wasn't gambling. He was playing pool with an older man whose caved-in chest heaved each time he banked a ball into a side pocket. Lori settled on a high stool at the end of the bar and ordered a beer. To the left of where she sat, on the back wall by the restrooms, was a shelf of stuffed animals, not toys but real animals that had been stuffed and mounted by Happy Jacks' owner, an obsessive taxidermist.

The area where cards were played was brilliant with fluorescent bulbs hanging from the ceiling, but the bar and back room were dim, lit by only the yellow light from a pair of weak hanging lamps and the animals' eyes, which glittered in the background like a short string of white Christmas lights. Lori twisted on her stool to watch the two men play. Game followed game. She was enthralled by the shine of Devon's black hair as he bent over the table, the lamp above swinging slightly.

Devon lost the last game and retired to the shadowed table where his two brothers teased him mercilessly until he crossed over to her.

"Would you like to play some cards?" he asked, and she laughed. It was so obviously not what she wanted. Back in the corner more laughter broke out. She was unschooled in the ways of flirting and didn't know to pretend, to join the brothers at the table and play prettily while answering Dev's questions on the side. She just laughed, pleased that he recognized her interest and returned it. He relaxed then, waved dismissively behind him, and leaned on the bar. He already had a glass of beer poured from the pitcher at the table, but he ordered a bottle with Lori and stayed to talk.

"Cards are funny?" he asked.

She shrugged. "I was hoping for a roulette wheel."

"Good way to lose money," he said. "Unless you're very lucky."

At that her foot slipped off the rung of the stool, and he caught her arm. He leaned in close; her hair brushed his cheek. Lori, high from her new-found job, the beer, the dim light of the bar, was missing her usual reticence. She half-closed her eyes in a way that tugged at Devon. Her mouth opened into a wide smile. Lori has extraordinary teeth, well shaped and a natural ivory white. In fact she has many pretty features. The interesting thing is that most of the time people don't notice them. She's usually biting her lip or frowning, and somehow her expression, pinched and forlorn, is all you take away.

Lori was lucky. Or thought she was. He called her. She went with him to Costello's for the music. Back at Happy Jacks he taught her to play pool. His brothers took turns dancing with her. Spruce taught her the Cajun two-step.

"Do you know a girl named Sarah Johansen?" Spruce asked her. "You could be sisters."

On the beach behind the old brickworks, Devon smoothed his sleeping bag out behind a wall of rocks and driftwood.

"Isn't it cold?" I asked Lori later. "Why don't you come here?"

But Devon liked the beach, and what he liked was fine with her. Their lovemaking had a sort of survivalist insistence about it. The freezing wind crept through the cracks in the driftwood and they tore at each other, digging themselves into a shallow hole with their passion. When she got home Lori's hair was always full of sand and grit. Her cheeks were wind burnt. She didn't even notice. It ticked me off a little, to tell the truth, that numbed glow she inhabited.

That April Dev went off fishing. He and his brothers worked a forty-foot trawler for Torkney Fleiss, the port landlord. They went out for salmon: coho and springs, chums and sockeye. Halibut sometimes too. Throughout the winter, they'd worked on the boat, but the last few weeks were a blurred rush. Lori was pressed into service running errands. It was a wonderful feeling to be needed, she said. She didn't mind them ordering her around.

"Next year you'll come along," Tim said. "We could use a spare deckhand."

"Like Sarah you mean," Spruce said laughing.

"Oh, Christ, if only," Tim swooned.

Lori blushed, ashamed of herself because she wasn't Sarah. Dev was down below in the fo'c'sle and didn't hear the conversation, but I was helping Lori pile boxes of gear on the deck and I did. I remembered Sarah Johansen, tall like Lori with the same long red hair and fine features. But where Lori can be gawky, Sarah was commanding. At Happy Jacks you could hear her laugh booming like a man's. Each year she rode her big bay pony in the Raspberry Festival parade. She'd dress as a cowgirl, shoot off a pistol of blanks, and throw candy to the children on the curb. I heard she'd gone off with a trust fund, a Californian with a big sailboat bound for Tonga.

Sarah was a town girl, born and bred. She and Dev had grown up together, although Dev was a few years older. Sarah had been in Spruce's class at school. Her exploits were legend to the Lund brothers, even before she got her hands on Devon. And once she did, boy, it was as if she'd stamped him *Property of* . . . Dev was like an old dog; Sarah was his randy carousing owner. It didn't seem to matter who she went off with—guys who frequented Happy Jacks or strangers who'd just cruised in on their boats for a restaurant meal and a morning at the laundromat. Night after night for weeks at a time Sarah would have a different partner. Then suddenly she'd be back with Devon, driving his little truck around filled with hay for her horses or stuck in a booth at the El Pescador laughing herself silly with all of the Lund brothers while Devon flushed with joy at her hands on his back, her silky red hair falling in front of his face obscuring his vision.

* * *

They were married in August in the field beside the firehall in Goldenridge, her mother's town. Before the reception began, his brothers put up the letters on the firehall's reader board: *Congrats! Devon & Lori.* Lori had read somewhere that only the first week of August was guaranteed sun in the Northwest, and it was a dream of hers to have an outdoor wedding. Families on Sunday drives or coming back from camping trips in the Cascades slowed and smiled out their windows, tooting their horns. On the lawn by the barbecues Lori said she felt like a one-woman show in her long white dress. She was lovely but awkward. More than once a drunken relative would come up for a bride's kiss, calling her Sarah. I'm Lori, she tried a few times, but no one listened. For a while Devon waved big exaggerated waves at the cars. He'd drunk glass after glass of beer and whiskey from a fifth his brother Tim was handing about. It was mostly his friends and family, many of them driving down from Anacortes and Bellingham, a few out from Seattle.

Lori's mother and stepfather and two brothers, Ryan and Don, were there too of course. Both her brothers single and unattached. Lori said her mother probably bribed them to be there, and I think she must have been right. Ryan brought his dog chained up in the back of his pickup. He kept leaving the reception to bring it the sodden ends of other people's hamburgers or walk it around so it wouldn't pee in the bed of the truck, though God knows how anyone could tell if it did. It was a bulldog and frightened Devon's younger cousins who ran to their parents shrieking, "Pit bull! Pit bull on the loose!" Drinks were spilled. Some potato salad landed on my dress leaving a grease stain on the right breast. Lori's mother, standing to my left, snorted as I scrubbed at the stain with the dampened end of a cocktail napkin emblazoned with Lori and Devon's initials. The stepfather, Mitchell, seemed hardly to notice the disturbance. He was more astounded that Devon and his brothers had come home early from fishing than he was concerned for his stepdaughter's happiness.

"Thousands," I heard him say. "They must be losing thousands."

I had to find Tim Lund for the wedding dance. He was the best man. I was maid of honor. We were supposed to dance together. I told him so.

"So," I said, "looks like everyone Lori and Devon have ever known is here."

"Almost," Tim said. His hand on my back annoyed me. It rested so lightly.

When the dance was over, Tim took off, leaving me alone on the raised pavilion as the next song started. Devon and Lori were clenched together. I noticed how their eyes never left each other and couldn't help cringing a little at what they must have imagined they saw. Devon and his wild woman brought to earth and held within his grasp. Lori and her safe haven. No good, I thought, no good can come of this.

The fire signal went off at that moment. The wedding was invaded by a fleet of pickups as the volunteers surged to their duties. Devon, drunk and flushed, was startled by the turn of events. He clutched at Lori to keep his balance, but he was too heavy for her, and to his brothers' great delight he fell backward and rolled under a table still covered with plates of half-eaten wedding cake. Lori, encased in her wedding gown, could not stoop to grasp his hand. She stood helplessly, her tiny white shoe beside his dark head, while the men bent with laughing.

On the first Monday of their married lives, Lori and Devon drove sixty miles south to look at a gillnetter called *Little Orca* that belonged to Sarah Johansen. She'd sent Dev a postcard saying it was time to sell. The postmark was blurred but the picture on the front was of a native woman holding coconuts in front of her naked breasts. "For you, a real deal," she'd written. Maybe *Little Orca* was intended as Sarah's wedding gift to Devon and Lori. Certainly Dev took it as such, though a feeling of hopelessness assailed Lori as they came aboard the weathered craft. Sarah had signed the card, *Love always.*

There are omens and natural laws on land as well as on sea. The Lund brothers would have done well to realize that. Dev taught Lori the basics: never leave port or shelter on a Friday; never allow a black suitcase to come aboard; if you must hand over a bar of soap, never place it directly in someone's hand, toss it into the basin instead; if your luck is bad, split open a coconut. There were strings of superstitions. He laid them out for her. He might have added one more: never allow a woman aboard who isn't your wife, doesn't love you, and yet owns the heart of your boat.

Through the winter they were happy if somewhat unsettled, living like squatters in the torn-apart cottage they were renovating above the bay. Then spring came. *Little Orca* was a treasure trove of unforeseen problems. Twice Dev tried to leave and had to be towed back in: a broken pump, rotted engine mounts. Finally in mid-April he was gone, late for the first run and anxious, a bank loan for the boat demanding the season be successful. A cousin had signed on, another friend would join them up north. Lori settled back into her solitary self, relieved in a way, I think, to be quiet again. The ghost of Sarah Johansen seemed to be losing substance. Salish Bay was like a bud, awaiting the crush of tourists, the overblown bustle of summer.

Then the week Dev left, Lori's boss, Karen, had a freak bike accident on her way to the restaurant. Lori called me and I drove over to Karen's house as soon as I cleaned up from the cannery. Karen's face was a mess of stitches. Worse, the palms of her hands had been torn open and embedded with gravel. Now they were wrapped in layers of gauze. Her left knee too had been affected. Nothing was broken but ligaments were torn, and she could not stand without crutches. I hung around for awhile filling glasses with ice water, fetching straws, until Karen said, "Forget it, Suzanne. I already hired a replacement."

And then there he was: Patrick, new to town. Another lost boy, I thought when I saw him. They showed up year-round in Salish Bay. Men in their thirties and forties looking like cute vagrant children. Attractive, lean and tan, they charmed, loved, and left. Hanging out in gangs like schoolchildren. And there was Karen, limping around the café's kitchen, exposing her secret recipe book to one of them, a stranger. She was still in a great deal of pain. Lori winced watching her face.

"I'm sorry for her," Patrick told Lori as he prepped for dinner the next evening. "But her bad luck is my good fortune. I don't usually have this much trouble finding work. I was getting worried."

I laughed. I could tell he wasn't the kind to worry about much. As he spoke he smiled and his eyes brightened. He was a tall man, terribly thin, all angles and hollows. His face had vertical lines running down it as if he'd once been folded. I'd come in after my shift at the cannery to check him out. In less than a week he was making modifications, baking bread for the café. Round loaves scented with different herbs, rosemary, oregano, sweet thyme. They were irresistible. I had been there ten minutes and already had made my way through half of one.

I came again the next afternoon and the next. It was a cheerful spot with Patrick there. Far better than with Karen doing her whirling dervish act. I was always in Karen's way. The dishwasher quit and I offered to fill in, cutting down my hours at the cannery despite Crazy Cox's threats to fire me altogether.

"Suzanne!" Patrick would say when I showed up. "We've been waiting for you!"

It was the way he said it. I forgave him for being a drifter. He was kind and worked like the devil, unlike all the pretty boys at the boat haven who seemed to think every hour working required another hour's latte break. And he kept away from the other lost boys. He rented an uptown room from old Mrs. Sayres, and other than her he never mentioned a single acquaintance in town. We all approved, even Tessa, who seemed to feel she had some proprietary rights since she'd been there the longest. It should have been Tessa who captured Patrick's interest. She was pretty enough and of the right vintage. If not Tessa, then me. I've been told I'm mature beyond my years. I've got a Grateful Dead T-shirt left over from the guy who lived upstairs. But, mystery of mysteries, Patrick admired Lori.

"Pretty dress," he'd say to her when she came into the kitchen, even if it wasn't.

He often stared at her. Once she was garnishing a salad, her head bent over the counter. He just put a plate up under the lights and stood gazing at her bare neck, the upsweep of her fair hair. When he saw me looking, he gave me the usual smile and waved a spatula as if to ask, "So what? Can you blame me?"

Patrick took to teasing her in front of us—me and Tessa and Conrad, the busboy.

"There she goes, winking at me again," he'd say.

"Does the fisherman know about us?" he murmured to Lori one night in the walk-in while they were shutting down the kitchen.

"Stop it, now," she said, but you could tell she didn't mean it. The way he talked, you might have imagined he was talking about a more forward girl, but if you were with them in the kitchen, the two of them working away quietly shoulder to shoulder, you knew it was her, Lori, he cared for.

Dev was strangely silent these weeks. April went by and May was waning before Lori got a short letter. One radio phone call. The friend in Ketchikan had not materialized. The fish were in hiding. He laughed, said maybe she should FedEx a coconut to him. Lori bought one, but I talked her out of it.

"It's a joke, Lori," I told her.

Then Dev's cousin's wife fell ill. He had to fly home. I ran into him at the Community Market, but he shook his head when I asked about Dev.

"Who took your place?" I asked.

"I'm not saying a word," he said grimly.

Each night Lori woke up gasping, then screaming from her dream. Finally that afternoon on the deck she let it all spill out to me—the water closing overhead, the wind that would not let her surface but kept pushing her away from the boat and Dev's outstretched hand. It seemed the dream gave her no rest, rolling toward her each time she closed her eyes. In the evenings at work she sometimes found herself without the strength to lift a tray, the dream replaying itself even then.

Patrick, who knew none of this, worried for her. He brought her vitamins and cooked special meals he thought would do her good. Gradually Lori warmed to Patrick's attention, taking on a vitality I hadn't known she possessed. She actually chattered and made biting jokes that took us all by surprise. It hurt to watch them, Patrick and Lori, but it felt good too.

In spite of Lori's newfound ease, Dev's silence rankled. She felt it when she came home and considered the unpacked cartons filled with wedding presents that lined the newly sheetrocked walls. She felt it when she drove to work and the waves beside the road bucked toward her. When she sat on the deck, when the wind picked up, when a child left a tiny pail of sand and shells on a table in the café.

"Suzanne," she said to me, "do you think I'm a greedy person?"

We were at Lori's, sitting at a table in the dining nook. Often after the constant rush of the café we were too wired to go home and sleep, yet too worn to face Happy Jacks. And so we would head to my place or, more usually, Lori's, for a glass of wine and a game of cards. That night I'd helped bus tables in addition to loading up the dishwashing conveyor, and I hadn't had much chance to eat the dinner Patrick had set aside for Lori, which I usually picked at as well. I drank the wine too quickly.

"You mean because you've amassed all this wealth," I said, waving an arm toward the stacked cartons.

"I want so much," she said. "It's not right."

"Of course it's not," I said, "and one day you will be punished. The earth will open and swallow you up. The *Recorder* will print a picture of a great gaping hole whose sides are strewn with wedding gifts: *Fisherman's Bride Goes Too Far.*"

Lori's eyes began to glisten. "Why doesn't he call?" she cried.

Out of nowhere I heard myself saying, "Patrick loves you, Lori."

She looked stricken. "Dev loves me," she said. "He does."

I shook my head. I started to tell her about the cousin, the guy in Ketchikan, Sarah. Lori covered her ears. I couldn't stop. I spat out all the images I had of Sarah and Dev together.

"You see," I said as calmly as I could, "he couldn't love you."

For the first time in our acquaintance I saw fury in my quiet friend. I managed one startled, "C'mon, Lori—" when the wineglass grazed my ear and fell shattering against the wall. In a moment I found myself outside, scrambling off the front steps in my bare feet, my sandals whizzing over my head, evidence that, despite the Lund brothers, Lori had not improved her pitching arm since summer camp all those years ago.

June 10th the Coast Guard found *Little Orca* drifting and brought her, empty, back into the harbor she'd left two days before. It was Lori's night off. When the news came she was sitting on her living room floor engulfed by newspaper packing and empty boxes. All around the room were shining objects—candlesticks, brilliantly patterned vases, small polished appliances. In her confusion she hung the phone up and dressed for work, arriving at the café just as the last diners were leaving. She came in through the back door, the same door through which she'd followed Karen. She grabbed an apron and started to tie it around her waist, but it was as if at that moment the news truly hit her. The thread of energy which had carried her from home to work snapped, and she stood there holding the loose apron strings, looking as if she'd just awakened.

She would not acknowledge Tessa nor Conrad nor, especially, me. One by one we left, leaving her alone with Patrick. He made her sit in a chair he'd brought from the dining room. He poured a glass of wine, placed it by her side. Then he sat on the floor across from her, leaning against the big freezer door, waiting. Finally she began to speak steadily in a voice only faintly high-pitched. All of it was about Dev.

Patrick swore he'd seen the wedding. In the kitchen of the café, when Lori described the yellow and red tent they had rented pulsating in the wind caught in the valley, he turned to her startled.

"I was there that day," he said. "That was the day I rode by Goldenridge."

He remembered the ring of cars and pickup trucks and the music that reached him when he stopped his bicycle. He remembered feeling wary when three men in tuxedos came out of the trees beside him. But they only wanted to offer him a beer. A cold beer on a hot day. That would have been Devon's brothers, Tim and Spruce, Lori told him. The third man might have been Keith, their cousin. Patrick didn't recall, though, seeing the huge flowerpots Devon's mother had placed at the foot of the drive.

"Big half whiskey barrels filled with lobelia and snaps?" Lori asked him. "Pale yellow pansies and that deep purple alyssum?"

But no. His eyes weren't able to take it all in. They were really pretty, those pots, Lori told him. Homey and elegant all at once.

For hours after the café closed, Lori spoke to Patrick of a perfect courtship, of love and passion and caring. She wove a marriage out of the whole cloth of a fairy tale. And Patrick listened and nodded. Around two in the morning she began to cry and he held her, heavy with his own longing. Then he felt her easing. Her body grew still, and when he looked he found she had fallen asleep. In the morning he took her home. His arms numb from cradling her through the night. He put her back to bed. She could not sleep enough.

She would not listen to me when I called. "Lori—" I'd begin and the phone would gently click and disconnect. Tim and Spruce arrived in town, as disheveled as a pair of drunks on a two-week binge. They stood on her doorstep, Tim's hand trembling on the front door he'd helped Dev strip and sand. Lori didn't want to see them. She sent Patrick to the door and sat at the kitchen table, listening. But Tim saw her arm through the open kitchen door and called out to her. "Lori, please!" Lori couldn't. She heard the frailty of Tim's voice and later an unaccustomed gruffness in Spruce. But she could not stand to see again Dev's eyes in Spruce, his lanky swaying walk when Tim turned and left. She could not say a word. Neither could they. What could they tell her? Could they tell her about Dev's second honeymoon, the bride of his heart fulfilling every fantasy? Picture for her Sarah slipping on the wet deck, piled deep with the droves of fish her false luck had brought? Or Dev as he reached out for Sarah, his hand just missing her? Didn't they know how, already, Lori had seen Sarah disappearing beneath the waves even as Devon, with an agonized cry, followed? Patrick offered them beers that they took and held like chalices in their hands. The two of them sat with Patrick on the front stoop of the house—their brother's house. They left him with papers for Lori and one photograph of a bare-chested Dev grinning like a madman on the deck of the boat.

Little Orca was Lori's now. Tim would have brought it down for her but Patrick said no. "Fill it